P9-CQW-268

j364.3   Bode, Janet
BOD

         Hard time

$16.95   39133

DATE			

DISCARDED

Brown County Public Library Dis
143 West Main
Mt. Sterling, IL. 62353

Brown County Public Library Dis
143 West Main
Mt. Sterling, IL. 62353

BAKER & TAYLOR

HARD
TIME

ALSO BY JANET BODE

*Death Is Hard to Live With: Teenagers and
How They Cope with Loss*
*Trust & Betrayal: Real Life Stories of
Friends and Enemies*

BY JANET BODE AND STAN MACK

*Heartbreak and Roses: Real Life Stories of
Troubled Love*

HARD TIME

A Real Life Look at Juvenile Crime and Violence

BY JANET BODE AND STAN MACK

Brown County Public Library Dis
143 West Main
Mt. Sterling, IL. 62353

Delacorte Press

9-5-6

BxT

Nov.97

39133

To Lucy Cefalu

Published by
Delacorte Press
Bantam Doubleday Dell Publishing Group, Inc.
1540 Broadway
New York, New York 10036

Text and illustrations copyright © 1996 by Janet Bode and Stan Mack

All rights reserved. No part of this book may be reproduced or transmitted in any form or by any means, electronic or mechanical, including photocopying, recording, or by any information storage and retrieval system, without the written permission of the Publisher, except where permitted by law.

The trademark Delacorte Press® is registered in U.S. Patent and Trademark Office and in other countries.

Library of Congress Cataloging-in-Publication Data
Bode, Janet.
Hard time : a real life look at juvenile crime and violence/
by Janet Bode and Stan Mack.
p. cm.
Includes bibliographical references.
Summary: Young people whose lives have been impacted by violence and crime, either as perpetrators or as victims, tell their stories. Also includes comments from concerned adults who work with these teens.
ISBN 0–385–32186–4 (hc : alk. paper)
1. Juvenile delinquents—United States—Case studies—Juveniie literature. 2. Crime—United States—Case studies—Juvenile literature. 3. Children and violence—United States—Case studies—Juvenile literature. [1. Juvenile delinquents. 2. Violence.] I. Mack, Stanley. II. Title.
HV9104.B53 1996
364.3´6´0973—dc20   95-40598
                                                                            CIP
                                                                            AC
The text of this book is set in 12-point ITC Bookman Light.
Manufactured in the United States of America
May 1996
10   9   8   7   6   5   4
BVG

CONTENTS

WARNING

I look around the room. There are a hundred or so teenagers sitting on folding chairs. They look like any other group of teenagers I've talked to around the country.

But here's the difference.

This group is a real captive audience. These kids are incarcerated in a coed juvenile corrections facility. They're not going anywhere for several months to several years.

Even the air feels thin and trapped.

A staff member tells me the kids sent here are runaways or car thieves, drug dealers, sex offenders, parole violators, the "gangstas" for whom death—yours, theirs, whoever's—is better than dishonor, no matter how small.

Tonight, though, they're quiet, waiting to hear what I have to say. They know that I write books for and about teenagers and that the books are collections of real life stories. What they don't know is that when I speak anywhere, I try to think about how my life experiences intersect with theirs.

When I look at this particular group, I'm forced to remember that I survived a crime committed by teenagers violent enough that, half a lifetime later, I'm still not free of the flashbacks.

An hour passes. At the end of my presentation, they've asked me questions, and then one, two, three, finally a dozen of them stop at the front of the room before being escorted back to the facility's ten separate units.

"Tell our stories," they all say.

"We're changing since we've been here."

"We're not animals."

Then a thirteen-year-old who looks eight says, "There isn't anything good about my life except I have one." Later I learn he'd been putting a starter pistol to classmates' heads, demanding money. His face shows nothing.

On the drive back to the city that night, I say to my partner, reporter-cartoonist Stan Mack, "Maybe we should do a book about these teenagers." He agrees that much of the talk we hear about crime and violence doesn't get beyond headlines and statistics.

This book would tell the stories behind the numbers. Who's getting locked up? What happens to them once they're inside? What do they value? Whom and what do they leave behind?

As long as people say crime and violence are beyond our control, that there's no solution, we give ourselves permission to walk away. This book could help call attention to the true dimensions of the problem in human terms. We've got to know whom we're dealing with in order to arrive at a truce.

THE SOUL OF THEIR STORIES

Our discussion is the beginning of eighteen months of research, writing, editing, drawing, and designing.

After receiving official permissions, I tape and transcribe conversations with incarcerated teenagers. We have an understanding. I'll retain the soul of their stories—their emotions and thoughts about life inside and out—but to protect their privacy, I'll change their names and certain details. As a further safeguard, I agree not to name the different facilities or even identify the cities in which they are located.

(I am, however, given permission to credit the poems; see the "Thanks" section.)

A year into the research, Stan and I return to the corrections center we first visited. This time we meet not only with the general population but also, separately, with the violent teen felons, the ones who've assaulted and murdered, torched buildings, and gone carjacking. For two days we conduct interviews in a cramped space within a communal TV area. Instead of stories told in words alone, some will have the visual force of Stan's pictures.

Behind a glass partition staff members monitor our movements.

One teenager calmly munches on a corn dog dinner while explaining how she tortured her best friend. Another talks nonstop in a gentle monotone, reciting events in which she was both victim and victimizer. A third begins to cry when asked what his mom was doing just before he pulled the trigger.

They answer some questions while ducking others. They recite facts but can't really say why they committed crimes or whether they'll go straight when released. Their tales are disjointed, unsettling, without warm, fuzzy endings. They're 1990s real.

Together, they make up "Inside," the first of this book's three major sections.

THE WORLD OUTSIDE

How far does the impact of the violent teen extend, I wonder. Teenagers on the inside remain tied to the world outside. They leave behind family and friends and, of course, their victims. I realize that in order for this book to be complete, I must gather those voices, too. That will be another section, "Outside."

I travel to public and private schools, talking to people in cities, suburbs, and the patchwork of small towns that covers the nation. I have discussions about juvenile crime and violence with members of a library teen advisory group, a writing workshop, a residential drug treatment program, a literacy project.

I meet with teenagers face-to-face, over the phone, in letters, and by e-mail. "Do crime and violence touch your life?" I ask. "Do you have any incarcerated family members or friends?" I discover the sisters and brothers, daughters and sons left behind, and I hear their pain.

Before answering my questions, the students often check out the reaction of those around them. For many this is an embarrassing topic. Then, suddenly and with resolve, a lone hand is raised. "My mom cried when my brother went to jail," says one student. "She always tried to teach him the right way. Now she says, 'He has to learn the hard way.'"

Then another hand goes up, and another. "My best friend's in jail, charged with murder. He was a ticking bomb that finally exploded. I pray for him."

"My dad's inside," says a student in a near-whisper. "He writes me, 'If prisons worked right, wouldn't we be closing them down?'"

They come up with questions for me to ask their peers behind double fences and locked doors. "What were you thinking when you did your crime?" "Do you believe in anything?" "What do you feel toward your victims?"

Individual teenagers volunteer to continue the conversations in one-on-one interviews. A suburban teen hands me a story he's written about his brush with the law. An urban teen wants to discuss the boot camp, a military-style prison, to which he was sent, and what has happened to him since his release.

Four young women with incarcerated parents describe how the experience changed their lives. They know that a high percentage of juvenile offenders come from families that have a parent who has been confined. One hints that she's resigned to that future.

INTIMATE ENEMIES

Back in the more public meetings we end up talking about how the roots of crime and violence run deep. A history teacher says that America is a high-noon-shoot-out, dying-with-your-boots-on culture.

I hear repeatedly, "Lots of people think it's cool to be criminal." There's also agreement that at times violence seems almost ordinary. "You forget to be shocked" is how a student puts it.

But you don't forget you are angry. The often-ignored truth is that the majority of you—even those coming of age in the most troubled neighborhoods—do not have violence in your hearts.

You do not turn to criminal activities.

Often, though, you feel alone in your struggle. You tell me that many adults have little idea how much violence routinely surrounds you. They don't know that nationwide more than half the high schools have instituted antiviolence measures, that half the high schools have started student assistance groups that meet to discuss how to deal with life's turmoil. They don't know that teenagers in prison and out are forever linked.

You are intimate enemies.

You are locked in an ongoing war in which most of you don't want to participate. While you want to trust your peers, you often fear them—with good reason. Teenagers are five times more likely than adults to become violent-crime statistics.

To compound matters, although more teens are being confined, ten times as many simply get away with the havoc they create. Students come up to me recounting their stories: "My ex-boyfriend and his three friends raped me. They passed me around like you pass a football," says a tenth grader.

"Kids abuse me and use me as their stepping-stone," says a visually impaired student. "My life is in my backpack and it always gets stolen."

When a teenager says he was "stomped down and robbed" by classmates next to a youth center, another student interrupts. "Me too," he says. "My jaw and two front teeth were broken."

All these crimes go unreported.

THE LAST "GOOD" CRIME REPORT

Finally, to place the stories I gather in a context, I look for the people I call the "Go-Betweens." That section focuses on adults involved with the issue. There's an Arizona dream analyst who works with incarcerated juveniles to try to help them develop remorse for their crimes, a Virginia teacher—whose husband is a repeat offender—who runs her school's student support group, and a California police officer who says, "Career criminals start as fourteen-year-old delinquents with problems at home and school, drug use, and gang connections."

I talk with media specialists, doctors, lawyers, prison officials, a judge, an institution guard, a recreational counselor, a rehabilitation counselor, a probation officer, and a juvenile justice researcher. They offer their own experiences, theories, and advice on what you as individuals and we as a nation can do to reduce crime.

From this range of people, I select six representative interviews to appear in the book.

Some stress prevention, rehabilitation, and job programs. Others advocate legisled parental responsibility, tough love, and more prisons. Meanwhile states from Connecticut to California, Florida to Michigan, are taking money out of education and putting it into corrections.

This book, I now know, is meant to be a kind of wake-up call. I hope that you, our teenage population, will read it, then pass it along to important adults in your life. Tell them that together you want to get involved in decreasing the violence and keeping the peace.

Tell them that the experts debating this issue agree on one point, their collective warning: Crime among teenagers is going to get worse.

The signs are clear. There's an increase in the sheer number of teens and a growing seriousness of their offenses. According to the most recent FBI crime report, from 1985 to 1995 the homicide rate among fourteen- to seventeen-year-olds soared 165 percent. As we move toward the year 2000 that report, chilling as it is, could be the last "good" one we'll see.

INSIDE

Becky, Age 17:
A HARD CASE

A DRUG

I'd love to be a drug
to constantly be needed
legal and illegal
to be the high people look for
no matter how hard the crash.

I'd love to be a drug
to aid and destroy people's lives
the worst destroyer
the best cure
the Good and the Bad.

I'd love to be acid
to show people a different way to see life
the colors and visions
the mind at work.

I'd love to be pot
to make people laugh
to make them eat
when they are too weak
to get people started on something more.

I'd love to be coke
to be the basis of a rich man
to be the reason why people get shot
to be snow white
to be a great high.

I'd love to be drugs.

Kenneth

18

SEAN, Age 17:

AMERICAN AS APPLE PIE

You've got to know that whole day is kind of a blur in my mind. As I remember, it started out just like a regular Tuesday in April.

I go to school. Talk to friends. After school two of them, Annie and her boyfriend, Jonathan, come over. We hang out in the backyard. We must have been talking for three or four hours. It starts to get dark.

We finally decide to run away again. This will be our second time. We have no set plans. It's just whatever happens. But we want a car.

I'm thirteen and a half.

I bring up the fact that I can shoot my mom and take her car. We don't talk about it for a while, but then I think I say again, "I can get my mom's gun."

"OK," Jonathan says, "but if you don't want to do it, I will. I'll go right through the front door."

At the time that hits a warning bell for me. Front door. On the street. I say, "No, I'll do it. Just dare me." All my life I've taken dares. It makes me ready for action.

"I dare you," Jonathan says.

I walk in the house and pretend I'm using the bathroom. Instead, I go in my mom's room and get the gun out of her sewing basket. I walk back to the bathroom, flush the toilet, wash my hands.

I go through the living room and get my mom's billfold. I take it into my bedroom and put it under the mattress. I open my window and show Annie and Jonathan the gun.

I put the gun between my pants and my hip.

I turn my radio on loud. I walk into the living room and turn on the TV. The CD player. I start playing with our cat, moving him into the dining room next to the kitchen.

That's where my mom is. In the kitchen. She has her back toward me. I pull the gun out and lift it up. Then I lower it.

She's eating a piece of apple pie.

I'm thinking, "I can't do this."

Then I get myself angry, thinking, "What about the time she hit me? The time she wouldn't give me what I wanted?"

I lift the gun back up.

I don't remember pulling the trigger.

I do remember the gun jumping in my hand.

I back into the corner. Then I run into my room, get her billfold, and hand that along with the gun out the window to Annie and Jonathan. I go back through the house toward the front door. I look in the kitchen.

My mom is lying on the floor.

I'm moving.

We jump in the car and start driving. Jonathan keeps bugging me, "Let me drive for a while."

"Sure," I say, and I pull over to switch. After that I just shut down. My mind blacks out. I don't remember anything until Jonathan is pushing on my shoulder, saying, "Sean! Sean! Wake up! How do you shift gears? There's a car behind us."

I can tell he's nervous. I look back and right away recognize it. "Look at the rectangle headlights," I say. "It's a police car." I'm scared half to death. "I told you to pull over into a motel. But you wouldn't do it. Now look what's happening."

"I guess the police saw me weaving a little."

"We better stop," I say. While we're talking, I'm trying to get the gun from under the seat.

The cop comes up and says, "You kids have driver's licenses?" When we say no, he goes to his car and calls for a backup. Other cops get there. They search us. They search the car. They find the gun.

"We're taking you to juvenile detention."

From that point on, they separate us. They do a test on my hands to see if I've fired a gun. I guess they've gone to my house and found my mom. One of the officers keeps asking me, "Sean, your mom's dead. You know anything about it?"

"Yeah," I say. "I did it." I think that's when the reality hits. I have actually killed her.

A PUNK

When I first got here, I was a punk. I didn't believe in anything. I put on a tough-guy image.

Now I've been inside four years. Other teens come in and out, in and out. I can see right through their images.

Sometimes kids drop it. I hear them talking in the day room, saying things about their parents. They just say the word "Mom," and it brings me back to my memories.

I have to live every day knowing that I killed my mom.

I miss her so much.

I had taken her for granted. Now she's gone. It's a void in my heart. I'm not even really sure why I killed her. I have reasons, but they're such small things. I can't believe I did it.

She was always a good person. When I was real young, the two of us used to go bowling. My highest score was 122, but I usually bowled about 110.

She was my single mom. She worked hard for what she got. She became the first union carpenter in our county. She taught me how to do stuff with my hands. She taught me values.

"Be honest with yourself and with others," she'd drill me. "In relationships, don't play games."

My mom taught me the basics of driving. "You can drive if an adult is with you," she said. Of course, I tried to manipulate that as much as possible.

We lived in a small town, but because we had relatives all around the country, I got to travel. We'd go visit them in Wisconsin, Kentucky, Arizona. On open stretches, she'd let me take the wheel. By the time I was thirteen, though, I just wanted to leave. Period. Back then I didn't realize that home wasn't so bad. I know there are people who'd love to have all I had: the nice bedroom filled with a TV, CD player, computer, Nintendo, a big bed.

I always wanted more.

My mom and I got in arguments over small things. It just built up.

SMALL AND BORING

I ask to rent a movie.

My mom says no.

I throw a tantrum. She comes in my room and says, "Don't ever slam your door again." I'm sitting on my bed, looking up at her.

As I stand up so we can be more eye-to-eye, I say, "I don't like you looking down on me." She takes a step back.

I can't get inside her head, but I guess she thinks I'm going to do something. She backs up and hits me in the face with a closed fist. It's like a mist comes over me. My eyes darken. I black out. Then I react. It gets me pumped up, my adrenaline going.

I swing twice at her. I hit her on the back. After that I run out of the house.

She follows me, yelling, "Get your body back in the house!"

I just stand there.

"I'm dead serious, Sean," she screams. She keeps cussing at me until finally I turn around, go back inside, and shut myself in my room.

The phone rings. It's Annie. "I want to run away," she says. "I need a place to stay."

"You can stay in our basement," I say. "Come on over in two hours. My mom will be asleep and I'll pull you through my window."

"Jonathan's coming, too," she says.

The next day they don't go to school. We have this hideout that we skip to. They go there, then I meet them after school. "I gotta get out of this town," Annie says. "It's small. It's boring."

Jonathan agrees. He wants to leave, too. "Me too," I tell them. That night I sneak them in my room again. Then when my mom's asleep, we go out my window.

We get in my mom's car, release the hand brake, push it a block down the road, and take off. We just drive and drive.

We drive to Cedar Falls, Des Moines, then all the way across the state line to Nebraska. Once we come back into Iowa, I drop them off at another friend's house. Then I start driving home.

It's a day later.

I start to get scared. I call Mom. "I've called the police," she says. "I want you home. Now."

I call my favorite uncle. "You got three choices," he says. "Go back home. Turn yourself in to the police. Go to this teen shelter I heard about."

"The shelter," I say, and he gives me the number. I go there; later that night, I turn myself in. They take me to the juvenile detention center. The next morning, my mom takes a bus down to meet me. She is so angry, she can't talk. She has this look, this very disapproving look, on her face. She shakes her head at me. Finally she says, "Let's go."

I get in the car next to her and we start to drive home. Halfway there, she pulls over at a rest stop and says, "Clean out the car. There's junk from Burger King, Taco Bell, Pizza Hut."

"Clean it out yourself," I say. I think that makes her more angry. We drive the rest of the way in silence.

A couple days later, my mom and I get in another argument. "You're not doing your schoolwork," she says. "I'm taking the TV out of your room until you show me your finished homework."

I grab the TV.

"Let go!" she yells.

So I do. I throw it across my bed. She catches the

TV by the cord and takes it to her room. She comes back and unplugs my phone. "I'm calling the police," she says.

I plead with her not to do that until she changes her mind. Within a day or two, the phone is back in my room. She gives me back my TV and even buys me cable.

She is always lenient with her punishment.

I think that's another reason I'm so self-absorbed. I can, I think, get away with anything and not have to pay for it. It has always been that way. I can't see why it will change.

BRUSHED BY A BREEZE

There wasn't a trial. I pled guilty to murder and they sent me here. In the beginning the staff doesn't make you talk about what you did. If you want to, you can, but they don't push it. Then after you've been here awhile, you have to write what happened the twenty-four hours before and after the crime took place.

If the staff doesn't think you're telling the truth, they make you do it again. And again. One guy told me he had to write his about fifteen times over six months before he stopped lying.

It took me the first year and a half of group therapy to realize that you've got to let yourself feel. It took me another half year of talking to apply that to myself.

The point they kept making was: You've got to understand what you did, why you did it, and how to prevent it from happening again.

They'd throw my crime in my face. We'd be agreeing how dumb violent acts are and someone would say, "Well, Sean, at least we didn't kill our mom."

Another person would be talking about having a hard childhood, being abused, stuff like that. He'd say, "I was full of rage."

The others would look at me and say, "But Sean, he didn't kill his mom."

"Hey, Sean, you got a God complex. You've been here so long you think you can't do wrong."

"Yeah, Sean, did you forget you murdered your mom? How wrong can you get?"

Those barbs hurt. They kicked me in the backside and got me moving. I learned I couldn't cover up my anger. I had to show it. I could do that and not actually hurt anybody. I can think about hurting someone, but I know inside, I can never do it again. There's so much pain from what I did, I couldn't handle it.

I began to learn how to cry.

This is my home now. I've grown up here. The people inside are my surrogate family. I try to keep my thoughts more on the inside. When I think about the outs—the world beyond the walls—the pressure starts.

I realize I can't experience the small things in life. I can't go outside. I can't feel the grass beneath my feet. I can't smell a new rain. I can't be brushed by a breeze. I can't touch a tree.

I think about the future. I will make myself have a future. Right now I'm trying to graduate from high school. After that I'm going to start college—that is, if the government doesn't stop the funding for it.

I can make myself somebody. I don't want to waste my time here. I want to make the most of it.

I have two goals. I'd like to be a marine biologist. I'd also like to be a doctor. I want to work at a profession that gives people something, that gives back what I took away.

I won't ever be able to bring my mother back to life, but I can honor her memory.

Sometimes it gets so hard, I think about killing myself. I get nervous knowing people on the outs judge me. They think I'm a monster.

But I'm still a person.

I have feelings.

And I am so sorry.

I can say "Sorry, sorry, sorry" so many times. Still, it will never change what I did.

I've been told, though, that I've changed a lot. I feel I have. I feel I am truly remorseful.

IF YOU ASK

If you ask where I come from
I have to start talking with a broken heart,
with a bat that has too much hardness

James

Angela, Age 16:

A BAD HAND

I'm Indian. I've lived on a reservation. I've lived off. And I've lived inside; this is my fifth time inside this one facility.

The longest I've been here is probably six months. This time it's three months with a parole date two weeks from now if I get OKs from the judge, the counselors, and my aunt. She's my legal guardian.

I'm here for my usual thing: theft and runaway charges. The day I was caught, I was trying to do good. See, I hardly ever go to school, but right then, I'd started back.

I had a doughnut and a Pepsi for breakfast, then went to class. The teacher says to this student, "Pick up that trash by your foot."

He says, "I don't touch nothing that's been on the floor. That's the janitor's job."

The room gets tense. The teacher lets it go and

says, "Everybody get out some paper and a pen." A guy named Tray says, "I don't have money for that."

She says, "Sell that leather jacket of yours to get some money."

Adults are afraid of Tray. Kids too. He sets the style. No one ever calls him on stuff. "F—— yourself," he tells the teacher. The bell rings.

"I don't need this," I think to myself. Me and a friend decide to skip. We go to the mall to shoplift. I take mainly makeup and some clothes. Bras, underwear, pants, a shirt, purses, and wallets. We don't get away with it.

I've been getting caught, and running away, for the last three years, since I was thirteen. That first time I didn't come home for a month. When I did, I was made to see a counselor. She heard my story and said, "I'm sending you to a residential drug and alcohol treatment center."

Two months into that program I ran.

I ran because I felt I needed to drink. I ran because I needed to use some drugs. I ran because in treatment I'd been talking about my life. It was really hard. And I knew alcohol and drugs could help smother my memories.

FAMILY OF FRIENDS

My mom's a prostitute.

We would move to anywhere there was work. We'd go to Tulsa and stay with one of her boyfriends. Or we'd go to Nevada, Wyoming.

She got me into prostitution and drugs when I was little. She'd take me to parties at this abandoned house. She started giving me alcohol, pot, acid, cocaine, and crack. At ten I was doing them all, and whatever else I could find.

Of course, so was she. She'd get wasted, get sick, and the next day she'd have a hangover. I'd have to nurse her. "You don't help me," she'd say, "you'll be more than sorry." She was right. She beat me bloody.

I was afraid of her. Once I tried to tell her, "Mom, I'm being abused by your boyfriend."

"Quit lying," she said.

When she walked in and he was molesting me, she walked right back out like nothing was happening.

There were times I felt I couldn't handle my life anymore. But I knew no one would rescue me. Instead, I kept telling myself, "When I get old enough, I'll move out. I'll quit being Mom's runner, quit doing drugs, try and do good for myself."

I was lonely. In my mom's world, there were no kids my own age.

The few times I showed up at school, the other kids were afraid of me. I found ways to do drugs on school property, and they knew it. I started to hang with older kids. They were in a gang. I was excited when they beat me in—they beat me up to initiate me.

For the first time I got close to people, mainly Joker and Rumble. They were like me; they had no one they could call a family to turn to. They believed me about being abused.

Every time I hurt, I went to them. They listened. They never judged me. They were mellow—unless you started something with them.

We went to parties all the time. We drank and we used—to get our mind off things, to ease the stress, or just to have fun. We were a family of friends. Joker and Rumble were two of the three most important people in my life. The third one was Duane.

A SPIRIT'S RETURN

I'll never forget the day I met Duane. I'm at a pow-wow competing in Indian dancing. I notice this cute guy. In between competitions, he's getting something to eat at a stand. I decide to go talk to him. "So what's your name?" I say.

"Duane," he says. "What's yours?"

"Angela."

I like that he's Indian, too. I like that he doesn't pressure me to do anything I don't want to do. And I can tell him anything. We are both into drugs, gangs, and trouble.

He's popular. Girls like him. That makes me smile.

For the next two years we break up and make up

more times than I can count. He's the only person in my life to say, "Angela, I love you. Will you marry me someday?" He even has roses for me, and some people that come and play music for us.

By then, though, I don't know how not to get into trouble. I get caught stealing, this time in a food store. I run away. I get some MIPs, minor-in-possession charges. I run away. I get charged with parole violations and more theft. I run away. I steal because I don't have enough money to get anything.

I go to juvenile detention. I go to an all-girls lockdown—where you can't go outside and you can't do nothing. I go to a lockup—you're doing time and getting help for whatever your crime is. I go to a coed correctional facility. And I go to four different drug treatment centers. Whenever I run from where I'm sent, Duane's the one I call.

"I can't take it any longer," I say. "Will you come pick me up?"

"Sure," he always says. "You can stay with me and my mom." One time after a couple days me and Duane fight, so I leave to look for Joker and Rumble.

I ask the first person I see that knows them, "Where are they?"

"Didn't you know? They're dead."

"When did it happen?"

"Yesterday. They were at home and a bunch of Demons did a drive-by."

34

If I was really their friend, I would have sensed it. I feel terrible.

Each night for a week, when I fall asleep, I have dreams where Joker and Rumble's spirits come back to me. They haunt me. For Indians, a spirit's return that way is scary. I should go to a medicine woman for a cure.

FLASHBACKS

What I see in my flashbacks are my memories from Memorial Day.

I had been out of drug treatment that time for about a month. I was staying at my aunt's. Duane called and asked me to come over to his place. He was having a party.

"No," I told him. "You know I'm trying to stay clean and sober."

"OK," he said. "But if you change your mind, just call me. I'll pick you up."

I didn't feel left out. I was doing good right then.

At two in the morning his mom called. She was screaming and crying. "Angela. Angela. Come over right away."

I woke up my cousin and got him to take me. I was banging on the door. I could see Duane's mom in the living room. Finally she let me in and I asked again, "What's wrong?"

"Go to the back porch and look."

"What do you mean?" I said.

"Go, go," she said.

Duane was lying on the floor in a pool of blood. He was shot three times in the back of the head. I didn't cry. I just stood there.

This guy had shot him when Duane was on the porch. That's all we ever knew.

I got home at six in the morning. I told my aunt, "We're having the funeral tomorrow."

"You're not going," she said.

"But this is the last time I'm ever going to see him."

"No," she said. "You've got to stay away from guns and trouble."

I went to his funeral. In the Native American way the funeral lasts three days. We dance. We sing. We eat. We talk.

I felt I had to be strong for his mom. She said, "Why weren't you at the party?"

I told her the story, that I was clean. That's why I wasn't there. "I'm happy for you. I only wish Duane was like that, too."

"So do I," I said.

HEALING

Lately when I'm not in treatment or detention or jail, I try to turn to my Indian ways. When I'm really down and I don't know what to do, I go see one of my elders.

They tell me old stories. Sometimes they take me to the sweat lodge. The sweat lodge is where you go to pray. You worship your great spirits. You meditate. With the heat, you clean out your pores.

Just before this last time in jail, I go to the sweat lodge. I know I won't like jail. I've been there so often already. But this time, I tell myself, "I will try not to be rebellious. I will try to cooperate with the program and the staff."

I am ready to go inside.

A couple months go by. Once more I'm clean and sober. I have a clearer mind. I can think about things and not forget.

For a while I feel I've been dealt a bad hand in life. The counselor says, "It is wrong for people to do what they did to you. You were the parent to your mother. That's not right or normal."

I start thinking, "Poor me. All these terrible things have happened."

Then one day my counselor says, "Angela, quit feeling sorry for yourself. It's not going to get you anywhere in life." I start to listen to those words. They make me stronger. Not right off, but I start to change. It takes time to heal.

The counselor says, "Phone call for you. It's your mom." I haven't talked to her forever. I don't know whether she's still a prostitute or dealing drugs.

I pick up the phone. My mom is crying, telling me she's just been beaten up. "I don't want to hear," I say.

She gets mad. "If you don't help me, I'm going to kill myself."

"Go ahead. Do it. I'm not going to cry over you anymore. I'm not scared of you anymore. I'm going to live my own life."

37

"You're a liar, a stealer, and a little whore," she says. "That's all you've ever been and all you're ever going to be."

"I don't have time to listen to your problems. I have my own problems and I need to deal with them."

"You're my daughter. You have to listen to me!"

"Mom," I say, "I'm doing good now. I'm going for my GED."

"You're stupid for going to school."

"You're stupid for not going to school."

I'm learning how to defend myself. When I say something about the abuse, she says, "You're wrong. That never happened."

"I'm right and I know it. Anyway, Mom, I've forgiven you."

She says, "I don't want to see you ever again. I don't want to hear from you ever again."

Before, I would have cried and begged her not to say that. But this time I only say OK and hand the counselor the phone.

I cry. I'm hurting, but I don't feel like hurting myself, like I would have in the past.

I start listening to the counselor's side of the conversation. "You have no right to tell Angela things like that," she says to my mom.

I can hear my mom screaming the way she always screamed at me. The counselor keeps talking. It feels good to have someone there to stand by me.

I know I can't be here forever, but this is a safe

place for me. I hope by my parole date I feel stable enough not to want to come back.

LIFE

My aunt called me. She said, "Some of your old friends are after you. They've been calling me, harassing me. They say, 'Tell Angela gangs are for life. We find her, we're gonna kill her.'"

They're jealous. They don't want me to succeed.

I didn't used to see much ahead for myself. Death wasn't frightening. To die was OK. I only liked money, 'cause there was a lot of stuff I wanted.

Now I think about a future. I'd like to start an Indian club for teenagers. Together we'll learn the Indian way—who we are and what we want in life. Then we could even teach white people what our culture is, and how to make more friends than enemies.

THE HAMMER AND THE NAIL

The hammer hit the nail.
The nail said Why did you hit me?
The hammer said Because I am a hammer and
   you are a nail
and a hammer can hit a nail because
that's what hammers do to nails
that's why they made hammers
to hit things with.

Robert

James, Age 14:

CRAZY DREAMS

I think about my family every day. About girls. About just driving around with my cousin Adriana. I think about being with my big brother, Ruben.

I think about being involved in sports again. Not having to have a gun or a bottle in my hand. And I think about my grandma cooking me a steak.

RUNNING THE STREETS

When I was born, my dad was in prison. My mom did drugs and dealt them. So did her boyfriend. He beat me and Ruben, and my mom too. Then he'd lock the doors and pass out.

We lived in a rough neighborhood. It was a junkie house, pretty much. Mattresses on the floor were what we had to sleep on.

By the time I was six, I was running the streets with Ruben. We stole from stores and got in fights.

Then one afternoon my mom got busted for

drugs. She was put on probation and had to go through treatment. They were going to put us in CSD, Children's Services Division. But my mom said, "No. I can find something better."

She took us to our grandparents, her parents. It was a total change. My grandparents were, like, "James and Ruben, you gotta go to school.

"You can't use.

"You can't chew.

"You can't walk around the town at night."

We ate dinner together at the kitchen table. There was a picture of the Blessed Virgin on the wall.

At first me and Ruben still stole. We still got in fights at school and got suspended. But then we started doing good. We were more like a family.

We played sports, wrestling, basketball, football. I played front guard. My grandpa came to my every game. I could hear him yelling, "Yo, James."

The other kids, they found out about my mom. "We've got moms. You don't," they'd say.

My grandpa said, "Leave it alone. That's nothing you can fight about." I wanted to make him and my grandma happy, so I learned to walk away.

When my mom got out of treatment, I guess we thought she'd come back for us. She was our mom. She had to love us more than she loved drugs. But she didn't. She was still into drugs. So what. She was never really there when she was there, anyway.

My mom's ex-boyfriend, I saw him once and asked, "Where's my mom?"

"I saw her at the Red Lantern a couple days ago," he said. I went to that bar, but I couldn't find her.

She never called.

She never wrote.

I'd ask my grandpa, "Where's Mom?"

He said, "We know as much as you do."

Two years went by.

BITTER TEARS

A week before football season ended, I get on the bus at school and Ruben isn't there. I ask one of the other kids, "Where's my brother?"

The bus pulls up in front of my grandparents' house. I get off and see that my grandma is crying.

Grandpa says, "Ruben's gone."

"Where'd he go?" I say.

"Your mom showed up. She gets to have you guys back from us. The CSD said, 'She went through treatment. It's her legal right to have her children returned.' James, you gotta go live with her."

"When?"

"Day after tomorrow," my grandpa says. When I start to cry, he says, "Don't worry. We get you guys on weekends."

"Well, at least that's cool," I say, even though by now we are all crying bitter tears. My grandma, my grandpa, and me.

Of course, the CSD lies. It doesn't happen. We can only visit my grandparents if my mom wants it. She never does. It's too much trouble.

That last day I don't want to go to school to say good-bye. I want to spend every minute with my grandparents. Finally it's time. I pack my clothes.

A caseworker comes. "Let's go," she says. And we leave.

DOING BAD

Ruben was only at our mom's and her new boyfriend's for three, four days and he was smoking again. In a few more weeks he started hanging with a gang, fighting, going to parties, coming home drunk.

I started doing bad, too.

Me and Ruben beat up our mom's boyfriend. After that we went to two different foster homes. I ran from where I was, like, five times. Ruben did the same.

We both kept telling them, "We want to go home to our grandparents." After a while they said, "You can spend weekends there, but that's all."

I was coming down the street when I saw an ambulance pulling away from my grandparents' house. The first thing I thought was "Ruben's been shot."

I ran inside and the neighbor lady said, "James, your grandpa had a heart attack. All the time he was saying your name."

By the time I got to the hospital, he was on the respirator. He could only look at me. I held his hand. He was crying. I wiped his tears. My grandma was in the room, and so was Ruben.

I called the foster home to see if I could stay. They

said, "No. We have rules. You have to be back this evening."

I stayed at the foster home for the week, then took the bus to my grandparents' for the weekend. As I walked down the driveway I saw my grandma. "What's wrong?" I said.

"Your grandpa died."

"It ain't true," I said.

"Ruben was holding him. The last thing he said was, 'Tell James I love him.'"

"It ain't true," I kept saying.

"But it is," Grandma said. "The funeral's in two days. The whole family will be here—your mom too."

My mom, aunts, cousins, some of my gang friends, we were all there. I went up to the casket.

I looked at him and said, "I'll see you someday." They closed the casket and put a flag on top of it. My grandpa was a veteran. At the cemetery they took the flag, folded it, and gave it to my grandma.

That night we went to my grandma's home. It was late. I got a phone call from two girls. I was out the door as I said, "I need to leave."

"Don't get in any trouble," my mom said. But I didn't hear her.

BEATEN IN

All my friends are getting beaten into gangs. Ruben too. I get beat in at a party. I know everybody there. They say, "You know what you are. You're Mexican. You're big. You should be in."

I'm beat in by twenty-four people. One eye swells shut. I'm hit on the head by a big bottle. I'm kicked. After that they hand me a forty-ounce. Then I have to go out and fight three people from three rival gangs, the Maniacs, the Hobs, and the Wizards.

There're, like, twelve cars of us. First we see some Maniacs coming out of a store. We drive behind them. I get out and walk up to the biggest one. I hit him. Next everybody jumps him.

We go and look for someone else. We drive to a grungy area where all the Hobs are, the hangout boys. There are eighteen, nineteen of them.

We go into the alley and beat up one, then another. When they start shooting, we drive off. There are guns blazing.

We go to look for a Wizard and find one at the mall. I just beat him up. Then I'm done. We all go back to our neighborhood and party.

I'm twelve, turning thirteen two months down the road. I don't mind the blood. I don't mind going out and coming face-to-face with a rival. In fact, I like it. I'm into the power.

It's a turn-on. Carrying a piece next to my body pumps me up. Just like in the movies.

After a while, though, I realize being a gang member changes my life a lot. I'm always fighting and always having to watch my back. My friends are getting shot, even my cousin Adriana. She's eighteen and has two kids.

Three of my friends are going to prison for killing these old people.

I don't care about my life. I figure I'm going to die someday.

PRISON OR DEATH

I'm in here for a fight, theft, possession of a firearm, and attempted murder.

We do a big group, about twenty of us and our staff. We open the meeting with the serenity prayer. Everyone says, "I'm an alcoholic," "an addict," "a gang member," or whatever they are.

When I first got here, I said, "Hi, I'm James, I'm a gang member alcoholic." Now I say, "I'm an alcoholic." That's my issue I need to work on.

Then we talk about feelings. Some pain in our life, like, back when we had a life. If we've been beaten or we fought, drank, vandalized, whatever. Then we talk about things that can help us.

I tell them, "I looked for the easy way, the easy prey. I didn't think, hey, they're mostly teenagers, same as me. Once we put a gun in some kid's mouth. 'Move and you're dead,' we said. Then we laughed, 'cause he cried.

"I know now that I don't want to keep hurting people. I don't want to live the life I used to live."

I get a letter from Ruben. "I'm back in prison," he

writes. "Shot eight times. I'm thinking about getting out of the gang."

That Sunday my grandma comes to visit. She says my friend Estevan was shot in the back with a .22. These two guys I grew up with had murder and drug charges against them in another case.

I write my homeboys still outside. "We're still friends," I tell them, "but we should all come together and not have to fight, not have to run the streets. We should stay clean. It's not worth getting sent to places like this. You lose your friends.

"I share a room with someone two years ago I would have killed. . . ."

One of them writes back. He says, "Man, are you crazy? You can't trust him."

I write my homeboy again. I say, "I need to be out of here to talk to my little cousins. They already know the gang signs. I need to tell them gangs are dumb. You don't need to fight over a color.

"Prison or death, those are your options. You go to prison for killing someone, or you're killed. Now I feel that I don't need alcohol and drugs to have fun. I'm back into sports, basketball, football, and lifting weights."

I want to be with my grandma. I want to live with her. I know I need the treatment. I'm doing it. My attitude is, someone can throw a CK, a cripkiller, around me and I won't do anything.

ONE CHRISTMAS

My grandma comes to see me again. She says, "Ruben might be sent to an adult prison, the one where your dad is." That makes me kind of mad, but that's the way things work out.

My dad, he's been in gangs, too. But what he's mostly done is been in prison. It's been six years this time. I've only spent one Christmas with him. I never spent a birthday with him.

I never played ball with him. I never went to a game with him. I never told him a secret.

I used to talk to him on the phone when he called sometimes when I was little. He'd get these crazy dreams that our family could be together. That'll never happen.

He's been told he'll never get out. He's "institutionalized."

I write my father and he doesn't write back. I tell him to write Ruben. That he survived being shot. "Two in his chest, one in the fat of his neck. He still has pieces of a bullet in his leg," I tell him.

I write my father again about a month ago, and I'm just waiting for a letter. Waiting. It never comes. It doesn't surprise me.

Everybody in my family except my grandma has been shot at. This is no way to live. I don't want other kids to have to go through this. And that's why I'm talking to you.

DOING TIME

Sitting in my empty room, staring at the wall.
Waiting for the sound of keys or a wake-up call.
Thinking of my friends and family that I left
   behind.
Daddy didn't see the trouble or maybe he was
   blind.
His little girl is locked up, it really breaks his
   heart.
I don't expect him to make a brand-new start.
I've been here many times before.
Once for cocaine, once for robbing a store.
Through all my trouble I can clearly see,
For a teenager jail is not the place to be.
But for some it's better than living on the streets,
Cuz they never know when they could find
   themselves 6-foot deep.
So the next time you decide to commit a crime,
Remember always, you may do some time.

Christy

Carlos, Age 21:

AN INSIDE JOB

DEAR NICHOLE,
REMEMBER ME? I'M 21 NOW. I'VE BEEN IN
PRISON FIVE YEARS. NICHOLE, I NEED A BIG
FAVOR BECAUSE I'M IN BIG TROUBLE.

I WAS PART OF A CREW
IN MY WING. WE DID
ILLEGAL JOBS FOR THE
GUARDS AND GOT
GIFTS AND PRIVILEGES
FROM THEM.

ONE OF OUR JOBS WAS TO ELIMINATE PROBLEMS THE GUARDS HAD WITH PRISONERS BY TAKING CARE OF THE PRISONERS.

GUARDS CAN'T RETALIATE AGAINST INMATES BUT PRISONERS CAN'T BE PROTECTED FROM OTHER PRISONERS FOR VERY LONG.

I WAS GIVEN A JOB TO REMOVE AN INMATE. I DID IT AND THE GUARD SET IT UP SO I GOT AWAY.

THEN I WAS GIVEN ANOTHER JOB. I TOLD THE GUARD I DIDN'T WANT TO DO IT. THE CREW CALLED ME A TRAITOR.

WHEN

When I saw you
I was scared to look at you
Now that I looked at you
I'm scared to touch you
Now that I touched you
I'm scared to hug you
Now that I hugged you
I'm scared to kiss you
Now that I kissed you
I'm scared to love you
Now that I love you
I'm scared to lose you

Presiliano

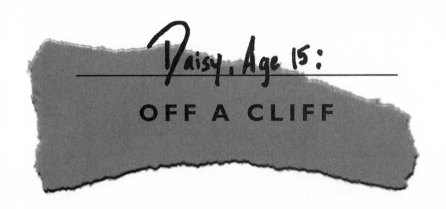

Daisy, Age 15:

OFF A CLIFF

I sit on my bed here in prison and write different years and next to them something important that happened to me at that age. Here's what it looks like.

MY LIFE LINE

AGE TWO: *mom kicks out my drug-addicted, abusive real dad*

AGE FOUR: *mom marries my brother's dad*

AGE SIX: *stepdad shoves dog poop down my throat when I refuse to clean it up*

AGE SEVEN: *real dad shakes my half sister to death*

AGE EIGHT: *stepdad starts sexually molesting me even when I hide in the corners*

AGE NINE: *start hearing voices & forgetting hours at a time where my friends & family tell me I act violent & strange*

And then I fall asleep, remembering the Ouija boards and cat spoons, remembering how me and my friends would draw the devil sign, a six-pointed star, and I'd sit in the center of the circle. There'd be a black candle. We'd ask for the devil to speak to us. I had such a feeling of power.

I felt I could jump off a cliff and not die.

Now I look at the door to my room here and in my mind, my imagination, I see the devil's face. I tell myself in the morning I'll get permission to put a picture on the back of that door. It'll be a calm setting, lush, with a waterfall.

PUMPKIN HEAD

My whole life all I've ever wanted to be was normal, like all the other kids. Instead, I have hardly any happy memories. But I do have something I'm proud of.

When I was thirteen, my stepfather was killed in a car accident. Instead of me breaking down, I became the mother to my mother and to my little brother. I cooked. I cleaned. I shopped. I was glad I was strong enough to do it. It gave my mom time to heal.

My brother's another story. I love him with all my heart. But starting when I was younger, I was confused. I used to hold pillows over his face. I'd spank him with a plastic hanger, tell him what he could and couldn't do.

I put the fear of God in him. I think he's still so scared of me that if I told him to do something and started counting, he'd do it.

At the same time I began getting into gangs. I was exactly thirteen years and nine months old when I shot a gun the first time. It was a rush. I was holding life and death in my hands. We shot at three gang members. *Pop pop pop.* That's the sound some guns make when you shoot.

Every gang has rules to live by. You might have a secret handshake and responsibilities, dues and meetings. If you violate any rule, it results in termination, either by death or a really severe beatdown—we call it a pumpkin head, since your head swells up.

When a member dies, maybe in a drive-by, you all go to the funeral and lay your rag on the casket. If anyone objects, it's an insult to the set and you're taken care of one way or another.

Any friendly association with a member of the opposite set gets you killed automatically. If you ever nark, you die. If you ever disrespect your color or your set, you are terminated.

And you have to get a tattoo.

MAJOR SINS

About a year ago, a month after I was initiated, I was walking down the street. I wanted to get high. I was wearing one of my gang suits. I had a rag wrapped around my ponytail and my 9-mm in front in my pants. Out of nowhere, six males in a rival gang pulled up next to me.

They pointed a gun at me.

"Get in the car," they said.

I was scared. They had the power. I got in.

I'm not sure whether they took me to a house or an apartment. What I know is they tied me to a bed. They sexually abused me. They beat me. I suffered two cracked ribs.

After three days they let me go—tossed me out of a car. I was naked except for this coat they gave me that came a little below my thigh. I walked to Kim's, my best friend's house. I told her, and we cried together.

This whole time my mom didn't know anything. She thought I was with Kim at a Christian summer camp when I was out committing major sins. Using. Robberies. Drive-bys. I lost control of myself and my life.

In my mind I saw myself as the one on the ground, bleeding, with all those medical people running around me. "Gang Girl Daisy Shot Dead" would be the headline.

Instead, after one robbery my friend Heather and I got into a fight and she stabbed me. Once in the leg, once in the right side. I had to be Life-Flighted to the hospital.

When the police came, I got charged with assault.

Heather told them, "Daisy was involved in a robbery, too. She acted alone. I was home at the time."

I remember looking the cop straight in the eye and saying, "I don't even know why I did it." He could see I was telling the truth.

But when I started talking about the rest of my life, about the voices, he said, "Kid, you're full of s——. You lying to get attention? What's the problem? Your mom ignores you?"

I tried to answer. He said, "You looking for excuses for the way you act?" I just shut down and stopped the words from coming. I didn't even care when first they put me under house arrest. Next I was sentenced to go to a foster home until a residential treatment center had a spot available for me.

After a month in the foster home, I ran away. I got caught and sent to a different foster home. When the cops found me, I said, "I'll run again."

"No, you won't," they said. "You're going to jail."

Within a day of being thrown into detention, I started a riot. My friend Ricki was being restrained by the staff. What that means is a lot of people, probably about nine, hold you down until you can't move. I remember just throwing aside the staff that was blocking the way. Next I was hitting and kicking the people hurting Ricki.

They tossed me on the floor and put me in handcuffs. By then Ricki was in handcuffs, too. But now she was only held down by one person. I started kicking that person in the face and throat, saying, "I'm going to kill you."

That's when they dragged me down four flights of stairs to the police car. I'm here because of my history of staff assaults and the robberies.

WALKING UNDERGROUND

In the other wings, you're given the privilege to walk aboveground to the school, to the dining room, to the gym, the weight room, the game room. But in the wing where I am, you have to earn those things. Until you do, you have to walk underground.

You also have to earn the privilege to interact with the rest of the kids. I guess you would have to be in lockup to understand the emotional bond you have with some of the people around you.

They're the ones who understand you have to sleep in a room with the door locked from the outside, eat what and when they say you can, speak when they let you, go to school wondering if the other students are going to try to get you in trouble.

I'm not used to this kind of life. I'm used to having a life. And I'm used to sex. I'm a player. The trouble is, it's against the wing rules to have any romance. You'd be spending more time paying attention to your boyfriend than to your treatment.

At first, I guess, I can't keep control of my desires. I have the need to know I'm liked. I write a note to a guy in my wing that says, "How would you like to go to bed with me?" He turns the note in to the staff.

I cry.

I haven't cried for nearly two years. Not once. But now that I'm inside, I cry. I stand by my porthole, this slot in the door where the staff passes things through to you, and cry and cry.

A staff who is still talking to me says, "Well, what's the problem?"

"I'm tired of playing games," I say. "I will do my program—the classes, the group therapy, the following the rules. I will succeed."

SURVIVAL GUIDE

Since I've gotten here, they've given me medication to help the voices in my head go away. Now I only hear them about twice a month, instead of all the hours of the night and through the day. It's funny, though. It's hard to adjust to them not being here, especially the little girl's voice that would cry, "I want my sissy, Daisy."

I've suffered years of listening to those voices telling me to do awful things. Even yesterday I hear one say, "Daisy, pick up this table and throw it out the window. You can do it."

I step away from the window. I walk over to my bed, sit down, and start taking deep breaths. I begin to calm down.

There's a new girl, Shelly, who's come to this

63

wing. She's great. We have become best friends. She's in here for the same crimes I am.

Together we wonder about the meaning of life.

"What is your purpose here on earth?" she says.

"To follow God," I say. "I keep the Holy Bible on my desk. I plan someday to read it through. I've always admired people who could read the whole Bible."

"Why did you pick it up in the first place?" Shelly says.

"I have no idea. I just walked into the library and took it off the shelf. I went to my room and read the first page. Sometimes I don't understand what it's saying, but so far my favorite part is the Lord's Prayer.

"Would you like me to recite it?"

"Go ahead," Shelly says.

"It says, 'Lead us not into temptation, but deliver us from the evil one, for God is the kingdom, the power, and the glory forever.' I feel that's what God did. He delivered me from the evil one."

In here, finally, my whole life has slowed down. Now when I find myself alone, with nothing to do but think of the past and of the future, I can feel the changes begin.

NO IDEA

Since Crime and Chaos run Wild in the Street,
We have to struggle to stay on our feet.
Dope Fiends Crying and Begging for a Rock,
Just to get high and be on top.
All the Kids are Skipping School,
Getting high and acting a fool.
What Do we Do about this Problem We Have?
Some people will cry, while others will laugh.
We have to help ourselves, and each other.
We have to love our father and our mother.
We need to help our land of birth.
We have to save the planet earth.
What is this world coming to?
I have no Idea—do you?

Rob

Mike, Age 16:

A REGULAR JOE

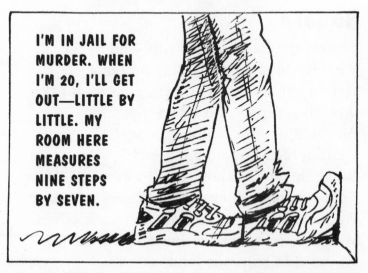

I'M IN JAIL FOR MURDER. WHEN I'M 20, I'LL GET OUT—LITTLE BY LITTLE. MY ROOM HERE MEASURES NINE STEPS BY SEVEN.

I KILLED MY MOM ON MOTHER'S DAY. WE WERE HAVING TAKEOUT. HER GUN WAS UNDER THE COUCH PILLOW. SHE WAS 39.

MY MOM TAUGHT US TO ROB STORES AND PLAY RUSSIAN ROULETTE. OUR HOUSE WAS FULL OF PEOPLE GETTING STONED.

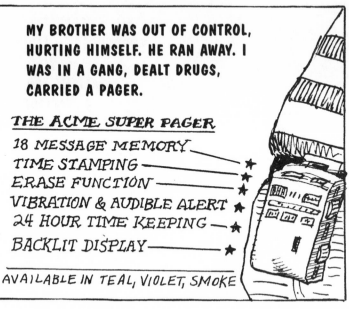

MY BROTHER WAS OUT OF CONTROL, HURTING HIMSELF. HE RAN AWAY. I WAS IN A GANG, DEALT DRUGS, CARRIED A PAGER.

THE ACME SUPER PAGER

18 MESSAGE MEMORY
TIME STAMPING
ERASE FUNCTION
VIBRATION & AUDIBLE ALERT
24 HOUR TIME KEEPING
BACKLIT DISPLAY

AVAILABLE IN TEAL, VIOLET, SMOKE

MOM SAID I WAS THE MAN OF THE HOUSE, BUT I BLAMED HER FOR GETTING IN MY WAY. I TOLD THE COPS A GUY SHOT HER.

I GET MAIL: SWEEPSTAKES, BROCHURES, MUSCLE MAGAZINES, LETTERS FROM A SPIRITUAL CHRISTIAN WOMAN.

A CHANCE

I had a chance
I don't no more
My chance has left me
It went out the door
My chance is gone
I can't find it no more
where are you chance
I need one more
Chance come back
through the door
please, please come back
I need some Help
give me another chance
to prove myself

give me a chance!!

Stephen

Collin, Age 16:

THE GLAMOROUS LIFE

In jail most conversations start with "What are you here for?" and lead up to "For how long?"

I say "Attempted murder of a cop" and "Three years eight months." On February eleventh I turned thirteen. A few days later I was inside. Now I'm sixteen, looking at seventeen.

By then, the new ones usually say, "What's it like here?"

I tell the truth. "I hate it."

Finally we just go off on tangents of war stories. Everybody does.

In my case I was about eight my first time in court. Me and Shane, my brother, and some of his friends took the shingles off a roof and started throwing them at each other.

Shane was four years older. He didn't really want nothing to do with me at that age. I was a pest. But he was my role model. Well, that day with the shingles, someone called the police. Three of us were charged. I was kind of excited this whole time. I felt, "Yeah, I'm up there with my brother."

I kept looking around at the weird people waiting in the halls. "Those are the rat heads," Shane said, "the narks in the reception area outside of court." At the time I didn't know what he was talking about, but I thought he was funny.

Finally me and my mom went upstairs to the second floor, where I met my probation officer.

They both lectured me for a while, until I went into court. The judge said, "Write an apology to the court, son."

BURNING REVENGE

Ever since I'm nine, I'm fascinated with setting fires. I'm not sure why. The first one is revenge to get back at my mom and Shane for I don't remember what.

I light my house on fire.

Instead what catches is a day care center. Shane sees what's happening and along with my mom's boyfriend gets the little kids out. I'm standing back, watching, with the rest of the spectators.

Another time I light a storage shed. I tell my mom, "The lady next door is the one to blame." The police don't question me about any of the fires until I'm caught setting bushes by a church. When they ask me about the other ones, I admit it.

This time I'm taken and put in a foster home. My foster parents let me know I'm in big trouble if I'm rebellious. "Collin, you're smart," they say. "Mellow out. Do the program. You earn points for good behavior, for doing chores."

"What's always made me have a name is my fighting," I say. "I fight at the snap of a finger. Over anything. I don't know why."

The structure and discipline make the difference.

I don't set any more fires. It's, like, a phase, maybe. I get in only one fight the fifteen months I'm there. My foster parents say I can go home to my mother.

That night, my first night out of the foster home, Shane takes me to a road strip where people hang out and fight. I get really stoned.

My mom's happy I'm home, but she says, "I have rules, too. I don't want you running with your brother and using coke, and you've got to be home earlier than two in the morning."

"No problem," I say.

My mom's too busy to notice. Within a month, we're evicted, move to a trailer, and I become a runner for her boyfriend, Justin. He's a dealer. I'm usually high every day. Justin teaches me how to weigh and cut drugs.

My mom knows, but she doesn't say much. I guess I'm just an out-of-control kid.

WIGGING OUT

I started fighting at school. I got kicked off the campus for smoking. At the school after that, I tried to stay out of trouble. It just didn't work.

I'd fight over a stare, a dare, a bump, or a stupid comment. There seemed, though, to be a pattern with the fights. I would get punished. The other people wouldn't. When the school security guard told me to go to the office, I was going to hit her with a bat. Instead the principal came up, so I hit him.

The next thing I knew, a cop was saying, "How old are you?"

"Eleven."

"We're taking you to juvenile detention."

"What's the charge?" I said.

"Assault and battery," the cop said. "But you're too young to be admitted with the general juvenile population. You'll stay in the holding cell till they decide what to do with you."

Foster care was the answer. Well, there I was at the foster home doing OK, brushing my teeth, when another foster kid pushed me. Then we got into it.

My foster dad came, separated us, and called the police. I was charged with assault. A court date was set. A special bus would pick us up and take us to a court-run school. That day I went to school, and after that I ran away.

Everybody knew I was running. Everybody at

school liked me. They were trying to help me. I found out where Shane was, in a shelter home getting ready for placement. He told me to get off the street. I turned myself in and went back to the foster home.

Time went by. I settled down some. Things started going good. I entered seventh grade. Then, November thirtieth, some friends persuaded me to run away with them. Three of us met in the morning just before school. One of the guys had a thousand dollars. He also had two guns, a .22 and a .38 revolver.

We agreed on our plan. "A carjacking and get out of town," I said. "If the cops pull us over, let me talk."

We were just walking down the street in the middle of the morning when a cop saw us. He started chasing us. We ran.

We shouldn't have run, but the other guys were new to the game. They ran. I ran.

I was wigging out.

"Hide," I said.

I had one of the revolvers in my pants. A cop grabbed me. I pulled out the .38 and was going to shoot him.

I had it in his face. We wrestled. He took it. I was hit twice in the head before I calmed down. By this time there were several policemen. They weren't playing no more.

I was kept in the juvenile detention center. Then I

had my trial. I got a court-appointed lawyer, Dick something. He was all right.

INS AND OUTS

Since I got here, all the time I think about what life would have been like outside. If I had gotten a car, gotten away.

I think there's two directions I could have gone. Part of me wants to lead that glamorous life—the freedom, the streets, the quick money. You know what they say, violence pays.

But I also have plans and goals. I want to go to college and be a lawyer. It depends on what the influences would have been.

I think mostly I would have gotten in trouble.

I think about what I am missing. I think about my family. I remember how we moved around. We had no stable place. Up until I was about eight, we were on welfare. When my mom got a job, I hated it. I did stuff to get her attention.

She'd try to keep boyfriends in her life. But when they'd want to father me and Shane, we resented it. Usually they were the ones that left her.

I think about my father sometimes. As far as I know, he's in prison. One time I was supposed to go to New York and live with him. He's a heavy drug user, mainly heroin. That's how my mom and him met. At parties. She wasn't an addict when I was born, but before that she was.

I think she quit because a friend of hers committed suicide while he was high. That scared her. Now she's a computer operator. She types in all the charges on people's credit card bills.

SCREAMING AND BANGING

I haven't seen cable for three years. I try to watch the news. I wonder, "What exactly is a crime?" It's mostly, I think, who's got the power. It's against the law to steal a soda. It isn't against the law for some boss to lay off two thousand workers.

I wonder, "What's the difference between gangs protecting their territory and the politicians, the Democrats and the Republicans, protecting theirs?" I like to know about what goes on out there. In my wing, though, most people aren't interested. They want to watch cartoons.

School is now the highlight of my day.

I read a lot. Newspapers. Magazines. Books. I like to read about Malcolm X. He's my hero. He learned to read in jail. He was able to see his mistakes and change.

It's stressful in here.

Suddenly someone gets out of control. A strip search with a guard looking for a hidden piece of sharpened aluminum. Next thing you know, someone's put in restraints.

Or they're suicidal.

I've seen two people hang themselves since I've been here. Neither of them died, but we got the point.

Sometimes at night, people'll be off screaming and banging until two in the morning, and we're right here. We don't get much sleep. The next day we're sitting in group talking about anger management or how masturbation is normal.

A "wing parent" teaches the new ones how to shower right, how to brush their teeth. We learn how to shave and to treat women as equal.

The wing parent goes on and on about "plain old common courtesy" and "how to have manners at the dinner table." We listen, but mainly we don't care. I count the cockroaches.

I think society's violent, and in order to get something you have to be aggressive—or violent.

For the rich yuppies, they don't have to be violent. It's not a problem. For me, it's something I have to do. I can't afford to turn the other cheek.

Right now I think I'm angrier than when I got here. And that's due to being incarcerated for so long. They've taken away my freedom and my teenage years.

The staff says, "Collin, do a reality check and stop with the victim role. There's a light at the end of the tunnel. You got sentenced as a juvenile. At twenty-one you'll be free."

About nine times out of ten, I hate the staff. I have to accept what they view as right and wrong. The staff parallels things; the punishment can be the same thing for simply being rude to being violent.

There's no in-between.

I don't take what I did lightly. I worry, "When I go back out, I'll have no idea how to act. How do I even order off a menu?"

If I'm in another fight, I'll be in here four more years. I worry some more. Who will I be then?

THE POLICEMAN AND THE KID

Don't steal that car, said the policeman.

Why? said the kid.

Because it is illegal, said the policeman.

Not if I don't get caught, said the kid.

You are going to have the whole police force after
you, said the policeman.

Then I will kill myself, said the kid.

Then we will tell your mother how you died, said
the policeman.

My mother is dead, said the kid.

Christopher

Susie, Age 15:

SO IN LOVE

I was going out with a guy named Jesse. Well, Jesse beat me. After he beat me, I would leave—when he let me.

I went through so much pain, but instead of leaving him for good, I'd do drugs until the pain would go away. This went on for a year and a half, off and on.

I was just so so in love with him. What more can I say?

I SO REGRET

One day my mom and dad were out of town for work. Jesse wanted me to steal their bank card and my mother's four-wheel-drive. I wanted to please him, so I did.

Now my ex-boyfriend Jesse is living with a fourteen-year-old prostitute that moved in two days after I got locked up in juvenile detention three months ago. I still love him and I always will. But never will be too soon to see him again.

Please tell my story so that other young ladies won't do what I did. I'm inside and Jesse's free. And even that little fourteen-year-old girl needs a life instead of giving hers.

Listen. Your life is important. You count, too. Don't give up on yourself. You don't have to. I have still more pain and I know drugs won't help. Plus I'm not the only one I hurt. I hurt my family, too.

Please remember this. No matter how much you love some guy, ask yourself, "Is he worth my life?" The answer is no! Don't do something you will regret later. I so regret giving myself to the beatings and to the drugs.

My final advice: Get help before it's too late.

GOODBYE WORLD GOODBYE

She stares at the gun
then back at the mirror

thinking should I
pull the trigger

What's there to live for
no one really cares

Why should I live, she thinks,
in a life that really stinks

Can my life get better
or should I just die

So she shoots herself in the eye
bye bye, world, bye

Monica

Sam, Age 14:
HERCULES GROWS UP

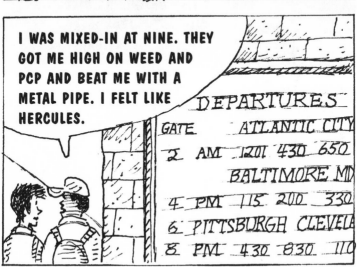

I'VE BEEN IN A DETENTION CENTER. NOW I'M ON PAROLE, GOING TO A GROUP HOME NEAR WHERE I LIVE.

I WAS MIXED-IN AT NINE. THEY GOT ME HIGH ON WEED AND PCP AND BEAT ME WITH A METAL PIPE. I FELT LIKE HERCULES.

DEPARTURES
GATE   ATLANTIC CITY
2 AM   1201 430 650
          BALTIMORE MD
4 PM   115 200 330
6 PITTSBURGH CLEVE
8 PM   430 830 110

MY GANG WAS MY FAMILY. I SOLVED MY PROBLEMS BY DRINKING AND FIGHTING. MY PARENTS WERE NICE TO ME, BUT I JUST LIED TO THEM.

I HAVE A GIRLFRIEND NOW. WE MET INSIDE. SHE'LL BE OUT SOON. THIS IS NOT LIKE ME, TO HAVE RESPECT AND FEELINGS FOR A FEMALE.

GO-
BETWEENS

THE INTERSECTION

GEORGES BENJAMIN, M.D., Chairman, Trauma Care, Violence and Injury Control Committee, American College of Emergency Physicians, Washington, D.C.

I run the emergency ambulance service for Washington, D.C., and I practice emergency medicine a couple days a week. Today's emergency departments are like MASH units in war zones.

We're treating gunshot violence, domestic violence, drug- and alcohol-related violence. And the victims of violence I see are younger and younger.

Many of you teenagers know this. You've been going to more funerals than proms. It's the adults who often don't seem to understand that everyone's kid is at risk. Even theirs.

Violence is spreading. This is a national problem and a national tragedy that starts with attitudes about what we accept as normal behavior. For too many people violence just seems matter-of-fact. They tolerate the fact that when one person's life is ruined by violence, it can ruin a whole family, a whole community.

They tolerate the fact that there's a lot of hate out there. They say, "I don't know what to do with these violent kids." They think that violence is an accident, an injury caused by a violent event, not preventable. They're wrong.

Still, nothing happens in this country until the public decides there's a need to change. The community—teenagers and adults—has to link up to deal with this issue.

Here are some suggestions of where to start, beginning with my own profession, where community problems and health intersect.

- Violence doesn't just happen and it's over. It's a chronic—long-lasting and recurring—disease. Kids come into the emergency room beaten up. Then they come in cut up. Then shot. Then fatally shot. In the past we've taken care of them medically, but not psychologically or socially.

  We understand that soldiers in war suffer from PTSD, post-traumatic stress disorder. Why would we think that kids growing up surrounded by violence would be any less vulnerable?

  We know what to do when people come in with chest pains and we think there's a heart problem. We talk to them about changing behavior. Stop smoking. Lose weight. Exercise. We

94

have to talk to these teens about changing behavior, too.

- The gun is designed to blow holes in things. It's an unregulated, unsafe consumer product. We know the technology is there to make it safer. Why don't we? We get caught in arguments between people who say "Get rid of guns" and those who say "Never." Neither argument has anything to do with making the product safer.

  Look what we did with cars. We recognized that cars had a potential to be dangerous and the human body is fragile. We did a whole bunch of things to make the car safer, as well as the process of driving it.

  We started driver-education classes and pushed to stop drinking and driving. With guns, the same message has to go out. They are dangerous. We are fragile.

- Parents should be a positive force. When a thirteen-year-old shoots a ten-year-old at two A.M., who's failing whom? Why were those kids out at that hour? Where did the gun come from? We have major efforts dealing with the trafficking of pornography to kids. Where is the major effort dealing with the trafficking of handguns to children?

  We know you can buy and lease guns. We also know that many of you can walk into your home and pick up a gun. The adult in your life should talk to you early and often about the dangers of guns.

Those of you in the inner city learn quickly how to walk the walk, watch your back, and not stare at anyone in a car parked next to you. Through example, adults should also teach you nonconfrontational survival skills, manners, and real respect. You don't take revenge on someone who accidentally steps on your foot because you see it as "disrespecting."

• Teenagers can make the difference. You know it's not a badge of honor that the U.S. homicide rate is off the charts compared with other industrialized nations. Yes, we are a competitive, aggressive culture, but you can channel those feelings in a productive manner. You can take advantage of community-based antiviolence programs run by the YMCA, the YWCA, the Boys and Girls Clubs, the churches.

Participate in your future. Go to town meetings, state and national hearings, speak on your own behalf about antiviolence programs and crime issues that touch your life. If you're eighteen, vote. If you're younger, tell your parents to vote your future.

Tell your school administrators that you want peer mediation and anger-management programs. From basic textbooks to school design and security, you want reinforcement to move you in a positive direction. If they say, "It costs too much," you say, "It costs a million dollars for health care and rehabilitation for one teenager shot in the back that results in a severed spinal cord."

I'm a member of Physicians for a Violence-Free Society. Violence-free is a goal. If you don't know where you're going, you won't get there.

BEGINNING OF
THE TUNNEL

CLEOPHUS GLASS, Deputy Superintendent, Spofford Juvenile Center, Department of Juvenile Justice, Bronx, New York

Spofford Juvenile Center covers a city block here in the Bronx. It has about eight floors wherein we have six wings. Juveniles are housed in dormitories, twenty-four per dormitory.

After children have been arrested and are taken to court, a judge makes the determination where they should be sent. Spofford receives youngsters ages ten through fifteen or sixteen while their situation is being processed. It's detention, not corrections.

Our daily population is usually about 290. We have approximately 6,000 children going through here each year. Fifty percent leave within three days. But the average length of stay is eighteen to twenty days.

Children come in and are searched. Their personal belongings are taken. We inform them of our expectations. They go through a comprehensive assessment. We check for everything from lice to bowel signs to any history of drugs or mental illness.

The new juveniles, here for the first time, are grouped together and oriented about the basic programs we have. We do that to allay their fears. They're often frightened. They want to know what's going to happen.

I've been at Spofford for thirty years. I started as a counselor, became a supervisor, and am now an administrator. Today I see not only youngsters coming back for the second, third, and fourth time, I see the younger brothers and even the sons of people who've gone through the system.

Our female population has increased, too. It's probably doubled just in the last ten years. And females are coming in with more serious crimes.

The residents are street-oriented. Their family structure—if there ever really was one—has decayed. More of them are basically homeless. And, yes, there is a breakdown in their values. They go for the quick and easy money. They sell drugs to get funds for those Nike sneakers and fine clothes.

The juveniles have this aggression when they come in. They have a strong sense of confrontation. Ten, fifteen years ago, after a juvenile was confrontational, he'd apologize.

Today there's no remorse.

They're fearless.

DAILY STRUCTURE

We have a sixteen-hour program. It's the daily structure. The children are aware of it. It's posted in the dormitories.

Each morning they're awakened. If the residents are going to court, they're up at six A.M. The others are up at six-thirty and prepare for breakfast.

Those going to court are placed on buses. The others go back to the dorms to go to group, where they talk about the expectations for the day. At nine they go to school until midafternoon, when they have another group session.

Then they have various recreational programs— outside speakers, sexuality education, parental groups for boys who are fathers and for girls who have children. We also afford them the opportunity to go to groups pertaining to religion.

Periodically we do contraband checks. We have security officers posted at the perimeters of the facility. We have counselors who monitor the juveniles returning from court. They are searched before and after seeing visitors. We have this structure to ensure their safety. There is less violence at Spofford than at most city schools.

At nine-thirty P.M. most of the youngsters have to go to bed. Those who have earned the privilege can stay up until eleven.

PREDICTION

We need to focus more on juvenile crime prevention rather than on incarceration. We need to flag those kids at the beginning of the tunnel, before they get deeper into the system.

We need more programs such as one called Family Ties, where instead of being sent to upstate facilities, juveniles and their families work with a family preservationist. In addition, we need more nonsecure detention programs—for example, structured group homes.

We need to expand the voluntary aftercare program that we have in New York and other states around the country. Here it's for children ages seven to sixteen. Those who enroll are rearrested at a much lower rate. The average bill for about six months' participation is less than what it costs to keep a youngster at Spofford for a week.

But I see prevention and youth programs being cut. I see no money in the pipeline. The teenage population is increasing, as is the seriousness of the crimes.

It's going to get worse.

INNOCENT OUTLAWS

RANDALL WATSON, Project Coordinator, Writers In The Schools, Harris County Juvenile Probation Department, Houston, Texas

I teach creative-writing workshops to kids inside. When I meet with them, they're awaiting adjudication—to be judged and sentenced. If they've been in here a long time, they've probably been charged with something like capital murder.

I can look at the charges, but I don't bother.

Often these guys are sitting with their foreheads down on the white Formica tabletops in the communal room. They do it because, maybe, it's their first time here. Or it's the worst crime they're in for.

They know they're screwed. And they're crying and trying to hide it from the other kids. I remember one kid, about fifteen years old. He would stay over in the corner sucking his thumb.

I get their poems where they swear they're going to obey their mom and they're going to go to church and they're never going to do anything wrong again

102

ever. Then they're out and back in four weeks for something like going into a high school and shooting up the lockers.

I have guys whose front four teeth are gold with their mother's and sister's initials engraved into them. I have other guys who show me pictures of their own kids. I say, "Well, where's one of the mother of your child?" And they whip out another picture, this time of the latest girlfriend.

"Are you going to marry her?" I ask. And it's, like, "Nah. No way." But they love their kid. A child is an accomplishment. It shows them they're a man.

While I work with them on their journal entries, their rap, and their poetry, I can sense their loneliness, rejection, and frustration. They don't necessarily acknowledge it, but it's there. Instead, they try to keep busy defining themselves by the anger they feel, by the adventure and thrill they get from the street.

In their writing they identify themselves as powerful individuals, bad and dangerous. They're bold. They don't care about the rules of the bureaucratic structure. They venerate the outlaw.

The outlaw is that individual who says, "F—— you. I'm tired of you telling me what to do. I'm gonna do what I want." Much of the American pioneer tradition is based on that concept.

But I don't want to be seeing them back inside. I want to be able to give them some knowledge. I don't know exactly what to say, but I use that quote, "Those who forget the mistakes of the past are bound to repeat them."

I say, "Remember that moment the first time you were ever arrested and put in jail? You were scared. It's OK to be scared. This is a scary place. Now maybe the next time you're outside with your friends, you can postpone—even for just five minutes—whatever it is that might send you back here."

I try to emphasize this point: Postpone action. When an impulse hits, say to yourself, "Not just now."

Then there are kids who walk in here and it's all gangsta rap. I can't get to them. They're too far away. I don't want to judge them, but they're lost causes.

MORE ALIKE THAN DIFFERENT?

There were two friends in my class. One couldn't read or write. The other wrote his poems for him. The message was "We killed someone. We are evil. Our lives are over."

I hear a lot of that. Now that they've done a truly terrible thing, they have to define themselves totally by the act. But deep inside they retain an innocence. They have the same feelings that other fourteen-year-olds have who have never stolen a thing or murdered anybody.

You kids on the outside should realize there may

be a lot less difference between you and your peers on the inside than you might assume.

Try this perspective. I ask you, have you ever snuck out, done things—drugging, tagging, trashing, fooling around—and then lied to your parents? Or have you fantasized shooting someone after you lost a fight in front of friends? How many of you have ever stolen anything in your lives? (You may lie, but most of you have.) And was it exciting?

The difference between you and these kids is that they're driven to extremes because they lack an understanding of another way.

SAVING LIVES

I feel tremendously close to the teenagers I work with. I identify with them. If I could be their big brother, I think I could save some of their lives.

But I can't do that.

In the end, I just hope that in the hours we spend together I have some impact.

TEENAGERS ON THE INSIDE ANSWER QUESTIONS FROM TEENAGERS ON THE OUTSIDE

THE QUESTIONNAIRE BELOW WAS DISTRIBUTED TO APPROXIMATELY 125 INCARCERATED TEENAGERS AGES TWELVE TO EIGHTEEN. IT WAS A VOLUNTARY SURVEY WITH A RESPONSE RATE OF 65 PERCENT.

Q.

What was it that drove you to risk your freedom?

A.

Freedom didn't even enter my mind. (Luke)

I liked to use drugs and it was easy to get a lot of money for a few minutes' work, meaning a burglary. (Gregory)

I had to show my mom that I could have power, too. (Melissa)

The thrill of knowing I was in control. (Kimberly)

To get out of a place I didn't want to be—home. (Mark)

On the outside, nobody cared if I screwed a duck or the king of England. Being paid attention to in lockup is nice. (Jennifer)

Q.

What were you thinking when you did your crime?

A.

When I started thinking, "What if I get caught?" I told myself, "Man, I'm slick. I haven't got caught yet." So I did do my crime and I did get caught. (Jorge)

I stole two cars off a car lot. I didn't think, "Will I hit a person or another car or maybe run into a tree?" All I had in mind was joyriding. (Eugene)

Innocent people are found guilty every day. I didn't do my crimes. I run away a lot, that's about it. I run away to be with the people the crimes I didn't do keep me from. (Tiffany)

When I did my crime it was more or less a challenge to have fun, like skydiving and seeing how close to the ground you'll get before pulling the cord. (Alex)

Q.

Do you keep in contact with your family and friends?

A.

Sometimes I call my mom. She's written me twice in four months. My dad abandoned me when I was two months. I have never seen him since. Some of my friends write, though, and give me good advice. (Samantha)

I keep in contact with my dad, grandma, and my cousin Tommy Jon. (Claudine)

Every once in a while my parents and grandparents come visit me. Also I get two phone calls every two weeks. (Kevin)

Q.

How do you keep from getting depressed?

A.

I'm given an antidepressant pill to keep me from the depths of depression and loss of hope. But not even the powerfullest med can keep me from crying at night when I'm alone with my thoughts and nobody to talk to. (Jennifer)

I don't. (Bobby)

It's hard because I lost my girlfriend while I was in here. I was with her for a year and a half. I still love her with all my heart. (Shaul)

Q.

Do you worry about getting raped or assaulted here?

A.

There are fights, but things don't get that out of hand. The staff protects us. (Gregory)

Not here, but I thought about getting raped in another prison. At night there were no rooms to be locked in and staff wasn't watching every second. (Lamont)

I just don't have fear anymore. I've been through it all at least twice. (Elisabeth)

Q.

What do you miss, deep down somewhere in your soul?

A.

I miss being out after dark. (Daimion)

Walking through the woods, touching the grass, climbing a tree, riding my bike, hugging my mom, swimming in the river, standing under a waterfall. *(Kelly)*

Being able to go anywhere without having to have an adult watching me. *(Joel)*

I miss having a mother around to talk to. *(David)*

Q.

If you could go back in time, would you do things differently? What?

A.

I would not even jaywalk. *(Alex)*

I would ask my mom why she came back in my life after seven years of being gone just to walk right back out again to go do everything she was doing before: whoring and drugging. *(Elisabeth)*

I would change my attitude and my friends and go to school. *(Rameau)*

I would listen to my mom and stay home instead of rebelling and running away. *(Kathryn)*

Q.

What do you feel toward your victims?

A.

Remorse, guilt, and pain toward my victims that I stole from or hurt. *(Concetta)*

Sad and sorry, but I can't change anything. *(Seth)*

Hate. *(Tiffany)*

I feel enraged at myself. *(Angel)*

What goes around comes around. *(Pete)*

Q.
Do you feel any regrets?

A.

My parents were too understanding. They could have been stricter in how they punished me before I got caught. *(Jeremy)*

No. *(Trevor)*

My family doesn't talk to me since the crime happened. *(Gregory)*

I regret using, whoring, and hurting people. *(Melissa)*

I feel so many regrets I could never list them. *(Lanny)*

Q.

What would you tell someone going to jail?

A.

Roll with the punches, look at things like an old movie, and remember that there is only one thing that can last forever—love.
(Jennifer)

Grit your teeth, bite your tongue, and hold on, 'cause it's going to be a bumpy road to recovery from life's wounds with many potholes along the way. (Alex)

Stop! Think about what you're doing. Hurting others is only hurting yourself in the long run. (Tommy)

Q.

Should there be a death penalty?

A.

Most definitely, because I believe in the Bible. Murderers and rapists especially should be punished. (Jasmine)

No. If somebody killed anyone I love, instead of the death penalty, they should rot in prison. (Lucretia)

If someone takes something valuable from others with no remorse, they should die. If they have remorse and can be helped and healed, give them the treatment they need. (Bobby)

I feel all gang-related people convicted of any major violent crime should get the death penalty. (David)

Sometimes I even wish I got it for the murder I committed. (Sean)

Why kill someone when you're sentencing them for murder? Two wrongs don't make it right, do they? Case closed. They should live with the guilt. (Gary)

Q.
Does it change your love life when you come out?

A.
Very much. Now I have to tell my girlfriend and eventually my kids what I've done— killed. (Clayton)

When I came in here, I wasn't involved with anyone. In here I have found love from another person, who happens to be a girl. We're best friends and I love her with all my heart.

113

She says the same. We will probably most likely see each other when we get out. (Kimberly)

You like girls more, because you haven't been around them. (Angel)

No. I will still be in love, just as I was the last time. Franklin and I were together the last time I was brought back on a parole violation. It hurts me to be taken away from him. We are so close and I miss so much about him and us. And it hurts me because I know it hurts him. (Toureanne)

Q.
What are your goals?

A.
My goals are to get out and be in a normal life again. After that I wish to become an NBA MVP and be on the All-Star Team and the Dream Team. (Leon)

I want to sing and worship God. (Jasmine)

I don't have any goals. (Cragg)

I want to get cosmetology training and write a book about my best friend, Carlina. She died

in a car accident three months ago.
(Samantha)

I want to go to college, get a degree, and be an interior decorator. (Lucretia)

My goal on the outs was to be a big-time drug dealer. Now I want to be an insurance salesman. (Kenyatta)

Q.
Do you believe in anything?

A.
You should treat others how you want to be treated. (Luke)

I have turned to God and let him into my heart after five years of worshiping his conflictor and oppositioner. (Jennifer)

I believe in the spirit of my grandmother.
(Concetta)

I believe there's a reason for everything. You just have to look to find it. (Trevor)

NO CHURCH CAMP

ANONYMOUS, Group Leader, Juvenile Correctional Facility

I've been a group leader for five years. I deal with teenagers whose self-esteem is in the dumps. First I have to get to the truth because they lie to you. I try to teach them morals, point out goals, and keep my eyes open for trouble.

We work on their education and why they're here. We'd like them to walk out of here knowing what a normal citizen should be like. And to follow the law.

Once they're out, it's their choice. They're aware of what they should be doing.

They also get physical activity. There's a weight room, a gym, and pool tables. They can wear their own clothes, but no camouflage, leather, or anything with a drug or gang sign on it. There's a page-long list of contraband, things they're not allowed to have, like tobacco products, aftershave, matches,

116

felt pens, cameras, large belt buckles, plastic bags, pornographic material, or bus tickets.

Mail is checked for contraband, too.

THE WOOL

My take on corrections for juveniles is that security is going downhill. It's teetering toward what kids want more than what they need.

For example, when kids get out of control, I think all facilities should have a mandatory strip search. Some administrators think a strip search is inhuman. I don't see it that way. To me it's a safety issue. A single-sided razor blade can do a lot of damage.

I know.

Here I'm one of the guys that does the search.

In any corrections facility safety and security have to be number one. Fun—physical activities—can't be as important. All of a sudden, instead of it being a privilege, kids start thinking that something like a pool tournament is their right.

I don't mind that kids get these treats, but I don't like them just handed to them. If facilities get too lenient, the tournament is on the teenagers' minds, not the treatment.

The bottom line is, we shouldn't have so many things for kids to do that they can forget about why they are incarcerated. I'm talking correctional institute. It shouldn't be church camp.

We have a ton of gang kids in facilities around the country. They're good at pulling the wool over the rehabilitation counselors' eyes. In my own experience, I've seen four success stories. That's about it. The others get out, go back to gangs, get arrested, go to prison—or come back to the same juvenile facility they left.

All states should have mandatory minimum sentences for juvenile offenders. Some states already do; the rest should follow.

In one state, for example, kids from fifteen to eighteen years old, if they commit certain crimes, they go to jail for a long time. Murder is 25 years. Manslaughter in the first degree is 120 months. Yes, that's 10 years. Assault in the first degree is 90 months, and so on.

Already people are trying to change that law, make it more lenient. I think mandatory minimum sentences serve as a deterrent. They're great. They should be voted in for kids down to twelve years old. I've seen twelve-year-old murderers with no remorse.

Kids are violent because they lack parenting. They lack role models. They go to friends for support. In order for the violence to decrease, the community has to enact minimum sentences, break up gangs, and come down hard on youth offenders.

A lot of teenagers need to be scared straight.

CHILDREN OF WAR

MICHAEL LEONARD, Community Service Probation Officer, Community Service Unit, Department of Probation, Brooklyn, New York

I handle the community service for the Department of Probation for Brooklyn, New York. Anytime people are placed on probation that includes community service, they have to come see me.

Together we go over their criminal record and where they're going in life. Oftentimes these aren't brainless people. And some of them weren't actually committing a crime. They're individuals who for some reason were in the wrong place and got pulled in with others. Or they got caught up in an argument, then were charged with assault. The intent to commit a crime wasn't there.

I try to place them at a site—a nonprofit organization or community-based program—where they can work for free. The average time ranges from 50 to 300 hours.

I'm also responsible for site development. I try to

convince people to let us send them volunteer labor. It's tough. When I walk in and they hear Department of Probation, the first thing they think is, "Criminal."

I say, "They're people. Give them a chance."

I'm here to help individuals rehabilitate themselves. I try to get them to take placements where they can train for something they'll enjoy. If they like what they're doing, they're less likely to return to crime. They might even find a job in that area.

We turn teenagers on to doing tutorial work. We have them learning different skills in hospitals, in churches. The Parks Department teaches them how to clean up a park, edge paths, clean sandboxes, that sort of thing.

We monitor them through site visits. We talk with the supervisors as well as the individuals. We want to hear both perspectives.

Probation is a sentence in the street; nonetheless, it's a sentence. Community service is a special condition of probation. If probationers don't show up, there is a series of steps we can take, including issuing an active bench warrant.

Currently I'm responsible for 570 cases per year. I have a community assistant and a clerical staff.

SEX, VIOLENCE, AND DRUGS

Crime does not discriminate.

When you don't get the education and the counseling you need, when you think you have no future, male or female, you're looking at trouble. Many of you numb yourselves from the reality of having to scratch to survive.

You do it through sex, violence, and drugs.

We're seeing more girls than ever before. More girls carrying weapons, too. They carry the same kinds as guys: guns, knives, and box cutters—the current weapon of choice. They forget its purpose is to open a box, not someone's face.

Prostitutes have changed. Years ago many of them did it because they needed to feed their family. Today, with the rampant use of ice and crack, they do it to feed their habit. But girls are also being arrested for murder, robbery, arson, for flying to Jamaica to bring back drugs.

It used to be that we picked up individual guys. They weren't thinking of options. They were just looking for the easy way out. That hasn't changed, but today these guys are hanging with their posse. There are more gangs now, and not just African American and Latino gangs.

The Russian teenager has his posse. The same thing for the Polish teenager, the Vietnamese teenager, the Chinese teenager, and on and on. It's a turf thing, where too many of you grow up feeling you have to defend yourself.

You are children of war.

240 NBA PLAYERS

What can we—you and I—do to reduce the crime and violence in your lives? In all of our lives? For starters, we adults need to work with you to give you a future. For that to happen, you may need to remind us of our responsibility. Then you have to be open to meeting us halfway.

Here's an example. The other day I was on the train. These teenagers came on, talking loud, cursing, scaring people.

I went over and said, "Listen. I need you to sit down and relax. You guys are making me afraid. I'm not afraid *of* you, I'm afraid *for* you. You don't know who else is on this train. You're like an accident waiting to happen."

They said, "Well, who are you?"

I flashed my shield. "This is who I am, but first I'm a person. I'm coming to you this way because I'd like you to consider your actions before you get in trouble."

As an adult, I must be responsible. If I see you kids doing something wrong, I need to say something. Then you should at least hear me out.

We need to be your mentors. And you need to grab positive adults to spend time with. That's how we pass down our customs, our wisdom, our spiritual values.

I was a Muslim until I was twenty-two. Now I'm a

born-again Christian. The teenagers I meet in my job often lack spiritual values. Their morals are not the same as those of the ones who stay out of trouble.

Hopelessness and despair exist. And if you don't have faith, that despair can carry you to your death. I want to speak a word of faith in your lives. Together we can make things better.

And together we should be practical. To stay away from crime and violence, bottom line, you have to stay active and involved in positive things. Right now, sit down and take a look at your strengths and weaknesses. Think about where you can go to turn those weaknesses into strengths and then build on them.

Knowledge and education are key. Reading is important. It opens up a whole new world. We must teach our children to read at every opportunity. Once you know how to read, volunteer to teach others.

Remember there are only 240 basketball players in the NBA. There are 28 million of you between the ages of twelve and nineteen. All of you are not going to be able to have a future as professional ballplayers.

Ask adults who have jobs that interest you how they got them. Starting now, what do you have to do to end up in the same kind of position?

Don't rule anything out, including law enforcement. A cop familiar with the families in a neighbor-hood is very valuable. Certain issues can be han-dled on the street level instead of by going through the system.

Many cases we're seeing don't belong here. Many communities are patrolled by people who don't un-derstand the customs and ways of those they're supposed to be helping. They can't differentiate be-tween the criminal and the citizen. You could make the difference.

Think about civil service jobs, teaching jobs, health jobs. But also think about owning and oper-ating your own business. From opening that first lemonade stand to teaching your friends how to play the piano, try to pick tasks that you feel you can really do. Then try to make money from them.

And, finally, pray.

5,000 KIDS

CHRISTOPHER BAIRD, Senior Vice President, National Council on Crime and Delinquency, Madison, Wisconsin

For twenty-two years I've researched and evaluated the U.S. criminal justice system. The National Council on Crime and Delinquency, where I've worked for the last ten years, is the oldest and largest criminal justice research organization in the nation.

We've learned there are misperceptions about juvenile crime and violence today. Because America's youth are being killed in record numbers, many people think that we're in the midst of an epidemic. They also think that the proportion of violent offenders among juveniles is much larger than it is for adults.

That's simply not true.

What *is* occurring is a randomness to the violence. Small to moderate-size cities, population two hundred thousand to three hundred thousand, are suddenly encountering things that never happened before, such as drive-by shootings. That's scary stuff.

Gangs historically had been limited to large metropolitan areas, Chicago, Los Angeles, New York. Now, for a variety of reasons, they've spread out, and the media are reporting it. Even though this type of violence is not rampant, it is new.

And people want it to stop.

LOCK 'EM UP

The current public attitude is to get tougher on juvenile offenders. Lock 'em up based on what they did plus what they might do in the future. If that means ignoring their constitutional rights, so be it.

In 1991 juvenile courts handled nearly 1,340,000 cases. Five years later the figure could be about one and a half million. Statistics show that growing numbers of these teenagers are being treated like adults.

Add to that the fact that minority youth are more likely than whites to be arrested and detained for the same kinds of crimes. Once in the system, minorities, particularly African Americans, consistently receive more severe sentences than do whites for the same offenses.

Some youth offenders are sent to *boot camps*, a term that has come to mean anything with a military style. There's not one shred of evidence they work.

Others are sent to facilities with double fences and razor ribbon on the top. Because of overcrowding, less programming is available to rehabilitate them.

Unless we do something about the behaviors that got them warehoused in the first place, we have an approach destined to fail. They return to the same circumstances, angry because of the way they've been treated, with no more skills than they had when they went in.

We're surprised that we have a high recidivism rate.

Politicians have to stop reading the tea leaves and thinking they're saying what the public wants to hear. They must be statesmen and say what the public needs to hear.

Politicians know what has to be done. We meet with legislators one-on-one and they acknowledge that the traditional approach of sending juveniles away to training school hasn't worked. It's not an efficient expenditure of money. On the political stump, though, they're right back to "I'm tough on crime and this is the way to do it."

The real way to do it is intensive community-based programs. (And the programs shouldn't overlook teen females just because they make up a small percentage—5 to 15 percent—of the correctional population.)

In these programs a worker goes to each home, picks up the kids, and takes them to the program, where they stay all day, sometimes as long as twelve hours.

They go to school, attend vocational programs, have counseling, are given opportunities for achievement and decision making, and learn the clear consequences of misconduct.

Then they go home and are either under electronic monitoring or physical monitoring by a staff that comes to their home or calls to check up on them. Their lives are controlled. They're getting the treatment, education, and aftercare they need.

That's not the way most states operate. At this time only Utah, Missouri, and Massachusetts are dealing with most of their youth offenders at a local level. These states still reserve their deep-end slots for the serious offenders.

There is always a place for residential programs. Very violent offenders have to be out of the community and incarcerated for a while. But even these juveniles need to be worked back into the community in a structured way as soon as we can.

FIVE REASONS

Why do we have such a high juvenile crime rate? Some reasons are clear:

- Historically, crime rates are higher in urban areas than in small towns and rural areas.

The United States is becoming increasingly urban.

- Crime reporting and its technology have improved. Also, teens tend to commit crimes in groups. The FBI statistics count the number of juveniles arrested, not the number of crimes committed. If five teens are arrested for a drive-by, it's shown as five homicide arrests, not one murder.

- The economy has gone through enormous changes over the last twenty years. You used to be able to quit school and go work in a factory. Now the employment prospects for teenagers without solid education have declined significantly. High unemployment hits younger and low-income workers the hardest.

- The combined issues of poverty, hopelessness, frustration, the easy availability of guns and drugs, and the day-to-day representations of violence in the media have to be factored in.

- Family disruption may be a cause or a symptom of teen crime and violence, but we can't dismiss the fact that a lot of teenage offenders come out of abuse and neglect situations. We see them in the child protection system. Then they graduate to the corrections system. Go through any of the files of kids in state facilities;

you get a remarkable sense of how bad their lives were.

It's estimated that each year 5,000 kids die as a result of mistreatment from a parent or guardian. Over 165,000 are seriously injured. Death at the hands of a parent remains much more common than being killed by another kid.

OUTSIDE

Facts

American teenagers are exposed to a lot of violence, and it's not limited to those who live in big cities. Seventy-three percent of students aged 12 to 17 say violence and crime is a major problem confronting teenagers. . . .

Exposure to guns is more common outside big cities: 57% of teens in suburban and rural areas say that someone in their household owns a gun, compared with 35% of those in small cities and 30% of teens in big cities.

Fifty-eight percent of all teens say their schools have taken antiviolence measures.

Greer, Emani, Jacqueline, Sarah
Ages 29, 16, 17, 17:

PARENTS IN CAGES

On a panel sponsored by the New York City Department of Youth Services and The Osborne Association, four young women talk about their experiences as the daughters of incarcerated parents. One and a half million children have parents inside.

GREER: When I was three, my father was incarcerated. At first I didn't understand what was happening. Then I was curious. The last time I saw him, someone, probably my mother, just said, "Daddy's going to be away for a while."

The adults in my life figured when my dad got sentenced to twenty-five years, he'd be out in five. He had no prior convictions. Everything was circumstantial. Much later we found out there was a letter from J. Edgar Hoover, then the head of the FBI, saying my dad was a "threat to society." They had a file on the whole family, where I went to school, everything.

I'm twenty-nine now and my dad's been out for a year. While he was gone, I grew up.

I graduated from elementary school. Junior high. High school.

I graduated from college in Atlanta, Georgia.

I got married, had a baby, and went to work.

EMANI: Right now I'm a sophomore in high school. I still remember the day my mom got a phone call. We were sitting in the bedroom. She hung up the phone and told me, "Your dad's gotten caught."

I was six. I said, "Caught doing what?" My mom was honest with me, but she never would tell me exactly my dad's story. In fact, only a couple weeks ago I learned what he was charged with.

Ten years later and he's still there. It's hard. Prison is not a good place to be, but I visit my dad. It takes between eight to ten hours to get to where he is. I drive with my mother. We go two times a year.

JACQUELINE: I'm seventeen now. The summer I was eight or nine, the police called my mom. "Your son's been arrested," they said. "We want you to come down to the station." She hung up, then stalled a lot. Like, she didn't want to go. I think in her heart she knew the police wanted her, but they didn't have enough evidence to arrest her. Finally my mom went, only she never came back.

For a week me and my three brothers stayed next door with our godmother. Then we stayed with my grandmother for about a year and a half.

I knew that my mom was in prison, why she was gone, but I wanted her to tell me.

She just said, "I did bad things."

My grandmother would say, "It's your fault, Jacqueline. You should have told your mom to stop."

"Stop drugs? An eight-year-old is going to tell her mother not to do drugs?" I said. "Mom was getting high all the time. She wasn't listening to me or anyone."

When things didn't work out with my grandmother, I was put into foster care. My mom didn't know about it until after I got in contact with her. Once she knew, she was glad and sad. "I'm worried," she told me. "You might get lost in the system."

SARAH: I'm a senior in high school, seventeen years old. Next fall I plan to attend college. My dad got out of prison this time two years ago. I helped him adjust and redirect his life since he's been released.

My mom was always pretty honest with me about why and how long my dad would be gone. It was for political reasons. He treated a woman who was shot by the cops.

When I had to tell people about my dad, it helped that that was the reason. It was justified.

Whether I visited him depended on which prison he was at. If he was close, I'd go once a month. But they moved him around. When he was far away, I went twice that year. Still, he wrote me often, and that was important.

I was five and a half the first time he went to jail. I saw him arrested on TV. That time when he got out he went underground. He was caught again and incarcerated again. He spent a total of eight years away.

GREER: My dad was part of the Black Panthers. We were not ashamed of his arrest. We were not ashamed of his conviction. He was working for the betterment of us as a family and our community as a race.

He went into prison when he was in his twenties. While he was there, he got an associate degree, a B.A., and a master's. He set an example for me.

Every other day I got a letter from him. He'd write stuff like "Education is the key to success.

"Persistence overcomes resistance. Hang in there.

"Once you acquire knowledge, no one can take it away from you.

"Focus on the positive experiences in your life."

My dad helped me deal with things even though he was away.

EMANI: To this day my father has rules for me. I can't go out with a boy till I'm thirty. And no sex till I'm forty!

My mom says, "If someone hits you, go tell your teacher."

My dad says, "Hit 'em back." That's what I want to do. Hit 'em back.

Many times I asked him, "What happened? What did you do?"

"I don't want to talk about it," he always said.

When I learned the truth, I felt betrayed. I was angry, too; still, I got through that quick. Now that I know the details, sometimes I feel I was better off not knowing.

He's in for felony murder. As I'm growing up, telling my friends "Oh, my dad's in prison for murdering someone" might not be the right thing to say.

JACQUELINE: My grandmother didn't want me to see my mother in prison, so I snuck up to the place. A whole bunch of nuns helped me get in. Go figure.

All the time I'd ask her, "Mom, when are you coming home?" She'd say, "Soon."

"Soon? How long is soon?" I'd say.

"Soon."

Well, she's out now. But in my life five years is not "soon." That's how long she was gone. Today she's a caseworker. We all live together, except one of my brothers is in jail.

What my mom went through is more in the open. I'm older, too. Remember, I'm seventeen. I have my GED. And I have a two-month-old baby. I feel I'll tell my child the truth. If he finds out later about my mom—his nana—it will hurt him even more.

Secrets cause pain.

GREER: My father was in for murder. They never found the weapon. He never knew the person. I don't think they would have been able to get a conviction now.

When people asked about him, I didn't go into details.

Now, you have questions, I'll answer them. But the reality is, the whole experience devastated me and my family. I still get teary-eyed when I think about all those lost years.

EMANI: When I was real little, I did tell some kids. After that their parents wouldn't let them play with me.

In junior high I didn't talk at all about my dad being in prison. I started saying, "My dad? He's down South. He's working." I wished so much there was someone I could go to and trust. Finally I had a therapist.

JACQUELINE: Kids are cruel. When they'd ask about my mother, I was embarrassed. Like Emani, I'd say different things. Sometimes it would be "My mother's on vacation." But you can be on vacation only so long.

I remember a teacher who asked, "Jacqueline, why are you telling stories about your mother?"

I said, "What do you want me to tell people?" I learned my lesson early. I knew whoever I told would judge me.

By the time I got to eleventh grade, I told the truth to my closest friends. If they couldn't handle it, they weren't my friends anymore.

SARAH: In elementary school one teacher took an interest in my father's case. He started a petition to get my dad health care. The teacher made it an OK thing for me to talk about my dad and what my family was going through.

In junior high many of my friends' parents were political. So again I was lucky. In high school I choose to tell some people and not tell others. But having a parent in prison impedes on your friendships.

JACQUELINE: Do I think I'm more likely than other teenagers to end up in prison? Not me. But my twenty-two-year-old brother is another story. He's always been a rebel. Getting high even when Mom was home. But then, so was she.

Once I went into his room. He was maybe thirteen. He was crying hysterical, "I'm a junkie!"

I was seven. I didn't even know what a junkie was.

When he was just fourteen, fifteen, he was robbing car radios. Now he knows the system better than the COs, the correctional officers.

I'm a girl, though. I had to be responsible for my little brother. It never came to my mind, "I think I'll go rob someone."

EMANI: I've never been arrested, but I have been getting into trouble. My sister's in jail now. So's my older brother. I only visit my dad.

Even after ten years, prison is still scary to me. My stomach hurts when I walk up to the gate. I pray the cops won't start on me. I'm afraid I'll flip on them.

After I'm inside, though, I see what I see. My dad has no responsibility. He can watch TV. He can play ball. It doesn't seem that bad. Then I start to worry. I'm always afraid someone will try to kill him. He has a big mouth and says stupid things.

Our time together is over so fast. And every time before I leave him, I say, "I love you." But how much did he love me if he did what he did? I cry almost all the way home. It's the worst.

But the truth is, I think it's real possible for me to do something that ends me up in jail.

GREER: I'm the only girl in my family, so they kept a closer watch on me. My brother's thirty-one now, two years older. He did time. It was his first arrest, a drug case. He did one to two years and is out now.

Any kind of incarceration is hard on the heart. I'll never forget visiting my dad. The COs, the correctional officers, were the worst people in terms of attitude. They're nasty.

And God forbid if an alarm goes off. They practically made you, the visitor, strip. They were afraid you were smuggling something. The way they'd talk to my grandfather, I hated that, too.

SARAH: I might be willing to go to jail for my beliefs. But now I think people like my father—who went to jail for his beliefs—are reconsidering what they did. When they were younger, they didn't think about the consequences.

I wrote poems to help me get through his time away. One was about being mad because he put the struggle first. I knew he loved me. But he sacrificed living with me. It still makes me cry.

You just don't want to think about your mom or dad living in cages.

My father was in a high-security prison. He was sick a lot. I wasn't usually frightened when I went to visit him. He was my daddy. But still, the prison had big gates. They clanked. They were meant to scare you.

JACQUELINE: My mom was at Bedford [a prison in New York]. Because of the work of the inmate

Jean Harris, they had summer programs where the kids of the women inside could stay for a whole week.

Of course, once I was there, my mom was like any mom. She'd try to control me. She'd say, "Do good in school. Don't drop out like me."

"Sure, Mom," I'd say.

"Be a good girl, take care of your brother, and don't give your grandmother a hard time."

"I don't," I'd say. "Gramma gives me a hard time."

Then she'd get all sad and say, "Please forgive me." And then it was over, time for me to leave. Every time, afterward, I was bawling for hours.

GREER: If you're in the same situation I was—if you have a parent or even a brother, a sister, an aunt, an uncle in prison—keep the lines of communication open. Remember, love can't flow through a closed heart. Peers can judge you, place labels on you. Write out your feelings.

JACQUELINE: My advice is that you don't listen to what your friends say. It just gets you angrier at your parents. It's hard because you don't know how it's gonna affect your home life, your education, your life. Find someone you truly trust. Scream with them. Cry with them. But remember, sometimes letting it out doesn't completely help. Don't give up.

145

EMANI: Just love your parent. The worst thing was, I stopped speaking to my dad for a short time. You have to be able to cry. A lot of boys say, "I'm a man. I won't cry." Forget it. Cry with your parent. Let them hold you. And you should let the adults around you know that they have to give you the room to slip, 'cause it's going to happen.

SARAH: Express your emotions. In a journal. With a parent. You have to let it out. It's also important to try to have some kind of support group. Try to get your parent or whatever adult is in your life to make it as easy as possible to talk about your feelings. And that adult should take you to visit the incarcerated parent.

"THE CRIME FUNNEL," DAVID C. ANDERSON, *THE NEW YORK TIMES MAGAZINE*, JUNE 12, 1994

Thirty-five million crimes—25 million of them serious—are committed each year in the U.S. Only 15 million of the serious crimes are reported to the police. The police solve 3.15 million of those cases, with 3.2 million people arrested. The courts convict 1.9 million defendants. 500,000 convicts go to prison. . . .

Younger criminals convicted of their first or second offenses commonly get off with probation or suspended sentences.

Renee, Age 18:
CONSEQUENCES

I feel a sense of danger at school. I'm careful. I don't want to be targeted. I don't keep anything valuable with me. Stuff is stolen.

This is a town of twenty thousand. There's no gang activity the way you hear about in cities, but there are kids who don't care. They start fights, especially racial fights. The police have been called.

It used to be a big deal to have these kinds of school problems. Now no students here are shocked anymore. In fact, some of them seem to be doing more dangerous and risky things.

When I listen to my friends, what they do, it sounds like things from the movies. Some don't think about the consequences. Some don't think they'll be caught. And some rely on being underage if they get into trouble.

THE CHASE

A couple of guys from school took one of the three taxis in town. A cop saw them and radioed in. Other cops chased them until the guys ran the taxi into a lake. After turning themselves in, they said, "It was just a little ride."

They got in trouble, but it was nothing much. Basically they were told, "Don't do that again."

Three other guys, Max, Jimmy, and Mitchell, went to visit one of Max's girlfriends in a mental hospital. Once they got there, they decided to break her out. A cop saw them, and Max said he told him, "We're here to see someone."

Yes, Max was telling the truth. But it was the truth for the moment, before they got the girlfriend and took off. There was a high-speed chase this time, too.

These are all friends of mine, and I'm reading about them in the newspaper—for taking a chance of ending up dead. When I talked to Max, he said, "We figured we could dodge the police." Then he started laughing about how fun it was.

I was so upset I said, "You only think about the fun at the time. You are risking other people's lives. What if you'd killed innocent bystanders?"

"That makes more room on the earth," Max said.

"We're talking about life," I said, "and it could have been yours. What if you'd ended up crashing the car?"

"That wasn't going to happen," he said. "Anyway, the only people in a little danger were just a bunch of cops."

"You don't think a cop could have family?" I said.

"Hey, my license was already suspended. I had to get away." And with that Max walked over to talk with some other kids. They were the kind who said stuff like "Oh, wow, what you did was a riot" and "I bet the chase was cool."

Most kids didn't say much at all. They were afraid. If you have opinions like mine, you hear, "Oh, Renee, you're too serious."

WISE COUNSEL

I haven't had a perfect life. I work hard. I believe that you can always make a situation better.

My mom's a teacher's aide. She says, "For too many teenagers, that work ethic just isn't there. They're only doing what's easy."

My dad says, "They expect to be the boss, not the stockboy."

I learned the difference between right and wrong, needs and wants, from the way my parents raised me and the guidance in the Bible. To correct someone you do not need to abuse them. You don't have to stick a child's hand over the hot oven to get your point across.

If you don't have a family unit, many of these problems are created. With no one checking over your shoulder, you only have your friends to teach you right and wrong. Teenagers can't give wise counsel to each other. None of us are experienced enough to guide and direct.

Starting in middle school, it's considered cool to come and go as you please. To tell your parents what to do. It can be good to have freedom, but you need to be balanced.

I'm a senior. I'm enjoying my independence, but I don't want to move out from the crib and then be stuck with bills. First I want to get myself on my feet. My dream is to be a psychologist.

155

BRANDON, Age 16:

A SUBURBAN LESSON

When I was fourteen years old, I wanted to party, be with my friends, and get girls. Especially get girls.

I had my eye on one girl. Her name was Gina.

One night I go to a party. A lot of people there are using drugs and alcohol. I'm straight-edge. I don't like to do that stuff.

Gina's at this party. She has been drinking and tripping on acid. Gina asks me to join her.

I'm faced with a dilemma. Should I go and get wasted in hopes of winning her affection? Or should I decline and risk looking like a fool?

Gina gives me a hit of acid and a forty-ounce beer. Soon we're outside, roaring drunk. The neighbors decide it's time for the police.

Since I'm a minor, the police take me into custody. They try to contact my parents but can only reach my sister, Karen. She comes to get me.

When my parents find out, I'm grounded until it's time to go to court. And while I'm grounded, Gina moves away.

I get arrested and grounded and don't even get laid!

This is the suburbs. The judge is lenient. He makes me attend a Saturday alcohol-awareness program. I tell him, "I've learned my lesson. In the future I'm going to try some other method to attract women."

Facts

Chicago, June 6 (AP) — . . . "Despite increased attention, violence continues to cause major health problems for adolescents," researchers said, citing several studies published in the past year.

In one study noted by the researchers, one in four young people ages 10 to 16 queried nationwide in 1993 reported being assaulted or abused within the previous year, and one in 10 reported being sexually abused or assaulted. . . .

In another study of suburban teenagers in Colorado and Ohio, 14 percent of girls and 44 percent of boys reported being hit or punched at school, suggesting violence is not limited to inner cities.

Being a victim of sexual abuse or assault is linked to high rates of alcohol use, sexual promiscuity, and other risky behavior. . . .

Marijuana use among eighth graders has more than doubled since 1991, the researchers said, citing 1994 government statistics showing an overall increase in drug use among teenagers.

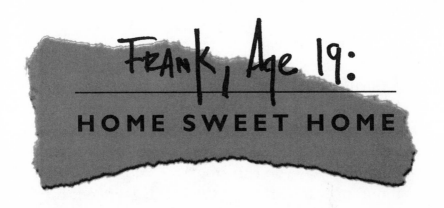

FRANK, Age 19:

HOME SWEET HOME

Jail is chaos.

A maximum jail has walls around it. A low-security is out in the open. I was sent to a medium jail. It was all fenced.

When I got there, the Man said, "Frank, the choice is yours. You can stay in medium or go to shock."

I didn't know what "shock" meant. When I asked the other inmates, none of them said anything good about it.

A jail friend, Taurus, said, "It's like the army, only a hundred percent worse. They make your life living hell."

"Most guys don't complete the program," another inmate, Rev, said. "Then you're sent back to prison to finish your bid, your time."

"You have no television, no radios, nothing," Taurus said. "Stay here. Do your time. Don't worry about it. We'll take care of each other."

"Listen," Rev said. "From five in the morning to nine-thirty at night the only time you can sit down is, like, in a group meeting or at school. And you gotta go to school. Then, say you make some noise they don't like, you gotta stand up and keep standing until they say you can stop."

I found myself with this little battle going on: the devious me versus the angel me. They stand, one on each shoulder, arguing what to do.

The devious me says, "Eh, don't worry. I got this plot for when you come out. This time you're not gonna do drugs, you're just gonna sell it."

The angel me says, "That plotting is going to bring you back to jail. That is not you. You're a smart person. You've got potential."

"You're not going to have to be in the street," the devious me says. "You're going to be the manager. People can just call you. When the cops come, you're going to be in your house."

Finally I thought, "Hey, look, man, this is not making it. If I stay here, I'll just become a better criminal."

I told Taurus, Rev, and some of the other inmates, "I'm going to shock."

In jail you have to keep a macho image. So when I told them my decision, I was put down.

"You're not gonna make it," Taurus said.

Rev was, like, "You want six months of hell instead of two years of sweetness? Just laying up, sleeping, and working out."

I heard them, but deep inside I knew my life was going down. I didn't have no type of routine. I didn't have nothing in my life. That's what always got me in trouble.

I wanted a chance to change.

SCARY-CRAZY

When I make my decision, they tell me I'll be picked up in a few days. From that moment on, I begin to psych myself up. I want to be ready for this rude awakening called shock.

The day the bus pulls up, I look around. Only a few of us are going. The few people that have the heart to take a challenge within our own lives.

I'm scared that I'm not going to make it. We're all scared. But we keep the image. Shock is still jail.

As the bus moves along, I start thinking about my family and about the first time I went to jail. I was scared then, too. Very scared.

I was sent to Rikers Island—that's in New York. I had to do six or seven days for attempted grand larceny. Then they released me. When I got out, I was happy. Back in my neighborhood, people were happy to see me.

I got the impression, well, that I was needed to keep on doing what I was doing. The guys in the 'hood made me feel, like, I'm a big shot now. I've been in jail.

Back then I didn't know this lesson: A man takes care of his responsibilities, his family, his kids, his home. Whatever the case may be, that's where his head should be. A real man has to do whatever possible for himself to change his life for the best.

The bus stops at the camp. It's January. The weather is freezing. There's snow on the ground. The door opens and three drill instructors come in screaming in our faces, "You #%^@&%**^! Don't look at us!"

"Sit up!"

"Eyeballs forward!"

It's scary-crazy. "What did I get myself into?" I wonder.

COCK-A-ROACH

"Yeah, you're bad!" the drill instructor yells. "That diddy-bopping walk? That's gonna be gone . . . along with your hair. Your head will be shaved. Bald. Every week."

The horn has just finished singing the reveille song. It's five A.M. I jump off my bed and stand in the position of attention. If I move, they'll drop me to do push-ups.

The drill instructor is at it again.

"You are not in society.

"You are not facing the corners.

"You are not facing drugs.

"You are not facing nothing.

"This is shock.

"All you got is your daily routine. Everything you do will be disciplined. If not, I will personally make you feel like a cock-a-roach."

I'm getting my first shock lesson. Their goal is to strip away our jail-street image and rebuild us into organized men ready to face reality. The only difference between this program and the army is, there are no weapons.

"Your weapon is your brain," the drill says. "If you're not mentally fit to go through this program, it's back to jail."

We have six minutes to do our bed, shave, wash our face, take a dump, get dressed into our PT gear, go outside, and line up into a platoon formation.

We have eight minutes to finish our food. The way we show how much we want, we put our hand up and show them. If we want a little bit, we open our fingers a little bit.

Well, during the day we are working. Going out to the mountains, chopping down pine trees. Those big things. Everybody be saying, "Let me get a lot of food."

The drill screams, "You don't finish your food, you will wear it. The rice, the juice, we will pour it on you! Down your pants. Down your shirt. You will stay like that until it's shower time."

Time management is a shock priority. Everything is timed. If we are late, we pay dearly.

"You will exercise in rain, sleet, and snow," the drill says. "You will exercise through the hottest weather. You will not walk. You will run. You will run until you change your attitude.

"You will change.

"Change.

"Change."

"F—— this," I think to myself. "I miss girls.

"I miss music, TV, dancing.

"I miss being able to phone, sleep, hang out, or just go to the bathroom on my schedule. I even miss going to the store.

"I miss being in charge of me."

I run ten miles and the drill screams, "That's not enough. I'm going to push you to the limit. I want three more miles out of you."

I want to leave. Go do my little two years. Relax. Have fun. Work out and do what I want to do.

In jail, you're not in control.

"I'd like my family to care about me, to sympathize with what I'm going through," I think. "I know I'm putting them through some painful days. But I'm in trouble. I have things in my life that are insane."

ADDICTION TO MONEY

As time goes on, I find myself becoming the person I was before drugs. My dreams come back into my life.

I want to become someone—a fireman, a doctor, whatever. I want to do something positive.

I want to go back to school.

It's like I'm thirteen again. I have put the last five years in the closet and locked the door. Now I'm opening a new door, too. Behind that new door is my recovery.

It's a spiritual awakening.

I know that on the outside I have nobody to take care of me but myself. I can't rely on my father or my mother. They're both addicts. My mother is also living with the virus, HIV. I've been parenting my parents.

I was brought up by my grandmother. But she had passed away before I was sent to shock. She tried her best, but things didn't work out that way.

When I was fourteen, I was already hanging out with older guys. They taught me how to rob. I saw other people getting money, and that's what I wanted. I had this addiction to money. Money gave me power.

We'd go over to Yankee Stadium to rob people. They used me as a decoy, then the older guys would come and take their money.

How much I got depended on how much we'd make. There'd be three of us and we'd split it into three. Sometimes it was a hundred dollars. Sometimes it was five hundred to a thousand dollars. Sometimes we just had to do one person. People had that much money they were carrying around. I didn't care about them any more than I cared about the people in my next career, the people I dealt to. All that mattered was the money.

I had to be organized with money, like a business-man. In many ways selling drugs is a skill. I had to know what I was doing. I had to be on point at all times.

I was safe as long as I was dealing heroin. Heroin turned me off. I saw what it did to people. I didn't like that down head. I always liked to be uplifted.

Cocaine was the drug that did that to me. Cocaine made me feel like I was it. I was in control. I was Al Pacino in *Scarface*.

When I started getting into cocaine, my life completely dropped. Everybody important to me got stung. When I was smoking crack or sniffing cocaine, I did not worry about anything. When I was sober, I thought, "Maybe I might get killed. Maybe the money isn't there anymore."

Most of the money wasn't mine, anyway. *They* were making the money, not me. I was spending my money on drugs.

I never took care of my top priorities, even though I was making money. In shock, when I'm forced to look at myself, I realize how deep I was into what I was doing. The reality of my life keeps smacking me in my face.

I think about it when the drill instructor says, "Shock's about teamwork. One person within the platoon messes up, everybody pays."

The first hundred times we hear that, I don't think, "Hey, they're teaching us to live in society. How to help our neighbors when they're down and out. How to realize that this person is not capable of doing something, so let's help him."

In the beginning when someone does something wrong, I get angry at him. We all do. Now I'm thinking, "Let's help get him through this program with us."

INSANE ENVIRONMENT

In shock we started off with fifty-six people, and only forty-one finished. Graduating was the greatest experience in my life. For the first time I knew that I succeeded at something powerful and good. And all of this, mind me, was done in jail.

The day we graduated, we did monkey drills, that's fancy marching. We got certificates. We got awards. I got one for being the person doing the most push-ups. I did 221 push-ups without stopping.

People's families were there. People were cheering. People were crying. I was proud.

And then it was over.

The bus pulled up.

It was time to leave.

Then reality hit. I was heading back to New York City. I was coming from a pure, disciplined environment, going back to the insane environment I left behind.

It was the angel me and the devious me arguing with each other. This time it was the positive me taking on . . . I don't know, the realistic me?

The positive me said, "You spent six months preparing for this day. You're ready."

"Is that right?" said the realistic me. "What about a job? What's going to happen when you have no money? And what about drugs? Are they really behind you? People in jail have problems so deep that other people are scared to let them back into society. When they get out, they're stigmatized."

"You are not completely OK. But recovery is possible," the positive me said. "If you get help, maybe outpatient therapy, people will see that. They won't stigmatize you."

The realistic me said, "You still carry that jailhouse mentality. People know. You're gonna end up back in the same place you came out of."

"You cannot go by what other people say or think or do," said the positive me. "You have to learn from your experiences. Use your experiences as a tool to excel in life. When you get off this bus into society, don't go back to the same places. Immediately try to do something. You won't get in trouble if you're going to school or dancing or playing basketball."

The bus pulled up to Yankee Stadium. I jumped off, looked around, and smiled. Home sweet home.

POSITIVELY REALISTIC

[It has now been two years since Frank got off that bus. He has participated in outpatient therapy, finished high school, done volunteer work, joined a basketball team, enrolled in college, fallen in love, "gone through a lot of trainings," and interviewed for more jobs than he can remember.

He has only worked for six months as part of a supervised release program. When potential employers look at his resume, they want to know about "this long period of time." He tells the truth—he was incarcerated. Now Frank wonders, should he lie?]

173

Facts

"HARD TIME FOR HARD YOUTHS: A BATTLE PRODUCING FEW WINNERS," JOSEPH B. TREASTER, *THE NEW YORK TIMES*, DECEMBER 18, 1994

Percentage of incarcerated juveniles in each type of institution in 1991:

OPEN—Halfway house, ranch or camp; rely on staff to control comings and goings: 42%

INSTITUTIONAL—Prison or school-type institution; rely more on locks and bars to control access to outside: 58%

AVERAGE DAILY COST for a juvenile in a correction institution; 1993 figures reported by selected states: NH $225, CT $198, NY $183, TX $53, DE $32, SC $17.

CRO, Age 14:
COURAGE AND HEART

My friend Giz was walking by himself. A bunch of kids started calling him a Herb, snapping, "You're a punk. You can't fight."

They wanted to take his chains and stuff. Giz wasn't going to have it. He ran and came back with people. There was a fight. That time it was just fists. But if they'd pulled a knife, showed a gun, Giz would have, too.

Sometimes people fight with fists in the beginning. But say Giz didn't feel he did enough to redeem himself. He might think he had to kill the person.

"It's all about respect and getting your rep up," Giz says. "If someone doesn't show you respect, you have to take it as far as you have to."

My friend Raymond says, "I don't care about other people's lives. Only my family and my friends.

If I'm in a fight and am beat down in front of people, I'd go back the next day and seek revenge. No matter how I get it."

In my neighborhood, you have a fight, you lose—now check this out—if you don't back down, people probably still give you respect. Then you don't have to get revenge.

If you lose respect, you gotta come back. There's just no way you can walk away from it. For me, I hope the other person doesn't want to use a weapon. But you can tell. They use phrases like "I got something for you."

"It's all about courage," says Giz.

Raymond says, "It's about heart."

They both tell me they're always prepared. They just don't bring the guns to school. The school has a metal detector.

BOX CUTTERS AND BODY BAGS

My mom had me when she was fourteen, turning fifteen. The same age I am now. My grandmother raised me. My mom went to school. Now she's doing pretty good; she's working two jobs.

When my father comes out on parole, I see him. But then he starts selling drugs again and he goes back in. I'm not embarrassed that he's in jail; I just feel, like, violated. He's been there since I was so young. I know him, but not enough to call him Dad.

I'm closest to my uncle. He's cool. I learn about the street from him. "If you're gonna go to somebody

176

else's neighborhood, watch your back," he says. "Look around.

"Don't ever walk by yourself. Go where there's a lot of people. Make sure nobody is trying to jump you. If somebody does, get that first person as hard as you can."

We talk about weapons. "You can make a weapon out of almost anything," he says. "You can use a box cutter, a screwdriver, a shaving blade, a fork, a butter knife. But, of course, the dangerous ones are the Glocks, nine-millimeters, things like that."

I collect gun magazines. I'm interested in them. I'm current.

My uncle and mom were born around here. She knows stuff, too. She tells me, "Don't hang around with drug dealers. If somebody is going to come around and shoot them, they'll catch you too, just 'cause you're with them. And don't start trouble. Only hit somebody if they hit you first."

In my neighborhood I've seen people hit with boards, laid out in their own blood, overdosed, jumped, chased, dodging bullets, arrested, dead in front of me, and taken away in body bags.

I've been scared, but I keep that to myself.

Last year I went to junior high right across the street from where I live. They had to send us around to the back door to leave each day. There were too many gunshots in front of the school.

The same thing with church. The church is on the corner, and the services are at night. My mom thinks something could happen as I'm walking by. I could get shot. She's nervous. "It's too dangerous," she says. "We won't go to church anymore."

I know my family loves me and cares for me. I have rules. I have to help around the house. I have to clean my room, go to the store, take out the garbage, watch my little brother.

I have to be in on school days at eight and on Saturdays, like, ten o'clock. Things happen when it starts getting dark. People come out to sell drugs. There are day shifts and night shifts. Night shifts are busier. All the crackers, the crackheads, come around looking for money to buy drugs.

LIVING FAT

Most of my friends haven't stayed out of trouble. The majority are selling drugs and acting crazy.

They go to school. They don't do homework, but they still get passed. They do what needs to be done to make it through. Then right after, they come out at three o'clock and they totally change. I got a couple friends, they go and steal cars.

Giz is a dealer now. He started out with a crew selling weed. He didn't like the money he was making. He wanted more. He started selling cocaine and crack on the corner, working for the big people on my block.

He was getting so anxious to make more money, he sold to a cop. Now he's in juvenile detention.

He wrote me a letter. He said, "Hey, Cro, don't ever go here. There are a lot of people trying to bone you up the butt. I don't want to be like that."

I'd like to see him, but they won't let me in. You have to be sixteen. It's funny. He's only fifteen and he's inside. But since I'm fourteen, I'm too young to visit.

I don't want to be in jail. I think part of the difference is that I don't have a lot of money, but I'm living comfortably.

What they can make in a day, I can make over the long run while they're in jail. I'm not worried about it. Most people want to live fat. Jewelry. Beepers. All that.

I don't need it.

But Raymond and another friend, Silvano, their mothers and fathers use drugs, so they don't have no income at all.

Raymond and Silvano resort to selling drugs not because they want to but because they wouldn't be able to live the life without that. Do you understand what I'm saying?

QUICK AND MYSTERIOUS

My friends call me by my tag, Cro. The crow's the only bird that flies in the night. That's why I picked it. I like doing things at nighttime. I'm quick and mysterious.

My mother doesn't want to hear about that side of

me. She thinks of the future. Nobody in our family has made it to college yet. "I want you to be the first," she tells me.

She worries I'll get my girlfriend pregnant. She says, "I'm only twenty-nine. I'm too young to be a grandmother."

I worry, too. If you ask me what's the one thing I'm most proud of, I'd say, "That I'm still alive."

Facts

As officials mull over a 28 percent increase in school violence this year, many push for what in city schools passes as a "high-tech" solution: more airport-style metal detectors. . . .

About 800 box-cutters were confiscated during the first half of this year. And a staggering number of weapons made their way into city's public schools during the 1993–94 school year: 7,254 guns, knives, box-cutters, brass knuckles, and razor blades were confiscated.

GROUP TALK

A TOP-RANKED, ETHNICALLY DIVERSE HIGH SCHOOL
IN THE MIDDLE OF URBAN SPRAWL.

DO CRIME AND VIOLENCE TOUCH YOUR LIFE?

ELTON, AGE 17:

A PROVEN MAN

It used to be that you had to lose your virginity to prove your manhood. Now it's as if you have to be violent, rob, deal, do drive-bys, to get respect.

AN ETERNAL FEELING

We moved to the suburbs for the usual reasons. For space, better schools, and safety. Still, my father pressed that it was our obligation to go back to the city and serve the community.

"When you give back," he'd say, "it's an eternal feeling."

Before we moved, I'd been an honor student. I had liked school. The first day at my new school, some white kids said, "You're black. You're not as smart as we are."

The principal called me into his office. "You're from the city," he said. "I'm not going to have any trouble in my school."

It was weird. I went from the top of my class to the bottom. My mama said, "Setting little goals and little accomplishments leads to bigger goals and bigger accomplishments."

My father said, "If you make the best choice in the environment you're in, you should have no regrets."

I was listening, but I wasn't hearing them. I started hanging out with the older neighborhood kids—Timmy, Ansari, and Ty. We'd play ball, go to the store, that sort of thing.

By the time I was in fifth grade, Timmy and the others would go to the store without any money and take what they wanted.

Then Ansari and Ty took a kid's bike.

A year or so later they beat up a guy and took his car.

The next time I saw them, they were talking about how much fun it was. At first I didn't comprehend what they were doing. But they were my friends. I wanted to be with them.

Once we were out just driving around. We stopped. Timmy and Ty jumped out. I didn't know what they were up to, but they came running back to the car and started driving fast.

ALIENATION

At the church we go to they call us the *Leave-It-to-Beaver* family. We even eat dinner together. There are other teenagers with parents that care, but the pull of the streets is just too exciting. They want everything now. They want to be accepted.

They break their parents' hearts.

But more often I begin to notice that I'm talking to my parents and my friends aren't talking to theirs. When Timmy, Ty, or Ansari do a crime, the important adults in their lives only say, "I'm disappointed with you."

"Disappointed?" What about angered, outraged, saddened? Your behavior must and will change. The little they hear goes in and out of their ears.

I'm getting more and more alienated from my friends. One day I'm sitting in the library reading a book called *The Black Panthers*. A white kid comes up and says, "Hey, is there an application for membership in the back?"

It offends me. I'm trying to educate myself. Why do I have to listen to this kind of thing? Of course, when I try to educate my black friends, they sometimes down me, too.

I'm walking down the hall and hear, "Elton, you're so black, you're two o'clock." I learn the dirty dozen.

When I get in tenth grade, Timmy, Ansari, and Ty, along with two other guys, rob a house. Maybe they would have gotten away with it, but one of them tells.

From that point on, Timmy, Ansari, and Ty are in and out of jail.

THE ANSWER

During that summer I went away for eight weeks. I come back and see Ansari on the street. "I'm trying to straighten out," he tells me. I hear he's selling drugs.

Another one of my friends is selling, too.

Two other friends rob a Long John Silver. By mistake one of them shoots himself in the leg. A police officer happens to go in there and ends up busting them.

Some little kids put on a bunch of jackets and run out of Macy's.

A kid down the street gets shot.

It seems like my whole neighborhood is deteriorating. Back at school there's a whole spectrum of attitudes toward the students who commit crimes. You have kids who want to be with them because they were in jail.

You have kids who make fun of them whenever their parole officer comes to check on them. More than one guy had to wear a house-arrest bracelet to school. They didn't get any respect from the other students.

Ty gets out of jail. He says, "The conditions inside are something else. We're treated like animals."

I think to myself, "I don't know if that's exactly wrong or right." What I do know, when he comes back to school, he has a hard time adjusting.

I wish I had the answer to what we should do to

people who rob, deal, and kill. I think some of them do need to go to a correctional facility.

Some of them don't realize what they do to their victims. That they are all hurt by the crime.

Still, to correct all this, really, it has to start when you're young and you learn respect. That's when you have to start figuring out how to deal with hostility and anger. You have to vent it on an activity—not a person.

I stop talking to Timmy and Ansari. They have no remorse. By now they're even scaring me. One day Timmy tries to get me into an altercation.

He's high and upset. "You're a chump," he tells me.

"Why? Because I don't want to be a loser?"

He wants to beat me up.

"Timmy," I say, "let's wait till we get outside of school. Getting suspended over an argument about nothing is stupid." With that he walks away.

THE INITIATIVE

What's going on shocks me. When I feel pressure, I go lift weights, play basketball, find something to do to get over those feelings.

I sit down and listen to music. I talk to people. When I express myself, they give me feedback. One friend says, "There's nothing worth tripping over."

If all else fails, I try to go to sleep. And usually every day I try to think to myself what I have accomplished.

I feel sad for some of these guys, for Timmy, Ty, and Ansari. They know what they're doing. They don't care.

I feel sorry for them, too. They should take the responsibility to help themselves out. Once Ansari and I are talking. He is telling me the reason he is being so evil.

"Because of the Man." That's the way he puts it. Actually he means the power of the United States government.

I ask him, "What has the government done to you physically? Mentally?"

He doesn't know what to say. Still, he is sure that the reason he is acting bad is because the government has dealt him a bad hand.

In reality, he and his family have a lot more than we have. "Ansari, you've got to stop making excuses," I say. "Take the initiative."

THE DIFFERENCE

I don't see those guys much anymore. Every once in a while Timmy and Ty honk their horns when they pass by. I lost contact completely with Ansari.

Now in my neighborhood you can hear a helicopter and police siren. There are drug dealers who deal out of their houses. I had a barber who lost his house and car when he got caught dealing.

I've started to volunteer at a home for battered children. I want to be a positive role model for these kids. I want them to learn there's another way to settle things besides violence.

A lot of my friends don't read much. They think writing is a punishment. My entire academic career I've felt I don't need a girlfriend to succeed. It's nice to have one at times, but study comes first.

I'm Elton. I need to do stuff for myself. I have to face problems. Get out rationally. I want to grow up and make a difference.

I'm a seventeen-year-old African American male virgin who was asked by three different girls to three different proms. And I have a scholarship to college next fall.

I don't have to prove myself to anyone.

Facts

"SERIOUS CRIMES FALL FOR THIRD YEAR, BUT EXPERTS WARN AGAINST SEEING TREND," FOX BUTTERFIELD, *THE NEW YORK TIMES*, MAY 23, 1995

The number of serious crimes reported to the police declined in 1994 for the third straight year, according to an F.B.I. report released on Sunday. But experts cautioned that it would be premature to conclude that crime rates were exhibiting a long-term downward trend.

Some scholars warned that the new figures masked a coming explosion in violent crime as the number of teen-agers in the population was about to rise. . . .

From 1985 to 1995 the homicide rate among adults over age 25 decreased 25 percent. But during the same period the homicide rate among 18-to-24-year-olds jumped 65 percent, and among 14-to-17-year-olds it soared 165 percent.

This is particularly alarming because the number of young people in the United States will climb sharply in the next few years, with 23 percent more teenagers by 2005.

Tanya, Age 15:

CHOICES

[A letter written to me by a teenager after she read one of my books.]

Dear Janet Bode,

This morning I checked out your book, Beating the Odds. I have already finished it. I am truly impressed. Not a lot of adults want to take things from a teenager's point of view.

I'd like to tell you my story.

When my dad was still

alive, but in the hospital, my mom already had a new man living with us. I don't remember much from that time. I was only six. But I do remember my mom not letting me go to my dad's funeral.

"You're too young to understand," she said.

To me, though, my dad was everything. He did all that he could for me and my brother.

Between his death and, oh, my eighth birthday, things were all right till my mom took off with Al. She left my brother and

me in a house where there
was no water, electricity,
garbage service or food.
My aunt found out
what had happened and
took us in. A few months
later my mom reappeared.
"Al was messing around with
a prostitute," she said. "But
that's OK. I met a man
named Pete."
"Where did you meet him?
" I asked.
"At a bar."
Figures, I thought. She
always drank and did a lot
of drugs. For the next couple
of years, my brother and I
lived with Pete and my

mom. He beat on her and got in a few fights with my brother. For a long time he never hit me, because I cried when he yelled at me.

Finally, though, Pete and I got into a dumb argument and he hit me. About a block from my house, he grabbed me by the wrist and ankle and literally dragged me home across the cement and all that.

He was yelling at me, "I'm your dad now. Your other dad is six feet deep."

The cops came, but they didn't do anything. Pete moved out and my mom gradually went with him.

She paid the rent at our house two months ahead, so I stayed there with my little brother. Still it was hard to go to school, take care of my brother, myself, all his friends and baby-sit enough to have money for food. As of a few weeks ago, we're with my aunt again.

Now this is what I want to say. All the time I lived with my mom I thought about how I could get attention. It was not by doing bad, gang-banging,

whatever. I decided it was
by doing good.
What my mom would say,
I did not let get to me. Like
when she told me that the
man that died when I was
six wasn't my biological
father. "I don't care," I
said. "He did all he could
for me."
It bothers me, though,
that my mom always told
me to respect her, love her
and be honest with her.
yet she's lied my whole life.
It kind of helps you lose
faith. The way she is, too,
has given me reasons to be
scared of love. If that isn't

enough, so many of my close friends have been killed or killed themselves that I have even more reasons.

I hope one day I learn to get over that. I hope I learn to love. For now, I write out my feelings and try to work through my problems that way. I'm a sophomore and I hold a 3.5 to a 4.0 GPA.

I gave up drinking without any type of counseling. Instead, I gave myself reasons to stay sober. I try to do everything to keep busy. I go downtown

and help homeless people.
I look at them as somebody
that has it a lot worse than
me. I realize how hard it is
for me. and I barely cope
sometimes. The homeless have
it even worse and nobody,
really, to help them.
I've discovered, its neat
to help people.
I know teenagers in de-
tention, in residential treatment programs, in boot camps
too. They have the same back-
ground as me. Life is about
choices.

Thank you,
Tanya

ABCs

ACTION

HERE IS A LIST OF ORGANIZATIONS INVOLVED IN THE ISSUES OF JUVENILE JUSTICE, ANTIVIOLENCE INITIATIVES, AND YOUTH WELL-BEING. IF YOU WANT TO TAKE ACTION IN ANY OF THESE AREAS, CONTACT THE APPROPRIATE GROUP OR GROUPS BELOW.

Centers for Disease Control and Prevention
Division of Adolescent and School Health
National Center for Chronic Disease Prevention and
Health Promotion
Mailstop K-33, 4770 Buford Highway, NE
Atlanta, GA 30341-3724
(404) 488-5330

Centers for Disease Control and Prevention
National Center for Injury Prevention and Control
Mailstop F-39, 4770 Buford Highway, NE
Atlanta, GA 30341-3724
(404) 488-4665

Center to Prevent Handgun Violence
(Handgun Control, Inc.)
1225 I Street, NW, Suite 1100
Washington, DC 20005
(202) 289-7319
(202) 898-0792

Center for the Study and Prevention of Violence
Institute of Behavioral Science
University of Colorado at Boulder
Campus Box 442
Boulder, CO 80309-0442
(303) 492-1032

Juvenile Justice Clearinghouse
National Criminal Justice Reference Service
P.O. Box 6000
Rockville, MD 20849-6000
(800) 638-8736
E-mail: askncjrs@ncjrs.aspensys.com

The Kempe National Center for the Prevention and
Treatment of Child Abuse and Neglect
The National Adolescent Perpetrator Network
1205 Oneida Street
Denver, CO 80220
(303) 321-3963

National Clearinghouse on Families and Youth
P.O. Box 13505
Silver Spring, MD 20911-3505
(301) 608-8098

National Council on Crime and Delinquency
Headquarters Office
685 Market Street, Suite 620
San Francisco, CA 94105
(415) 896-6223

National Crime Prevention Council
1700 K Street, NW, second floor
Washington, DC 20006
(202) 466-6272

National Institute for Dispute Resolution
1726 M Street, NW, Suite 500
Washington, DC 20036
(202) 466-4764
E-mail: nidr@igc.apc.org
conflictnet@igc.apc.org

The National Network for Youth
1319 F Street, NW, Suite 401
Washington, DC 20004
(formerly National Network of Runaway and Youth
Services, Inc.)
(202) 783-7949
E-mail: nn4youth@aol.com

The National Runaway Switchboard
(800) 621-4000

The Osborne Association
809 Westchester Avenue
Bronx, NY 10455
(718) 842-0500

Physicians for a Violence-Free Society
P.O. Box 35528
Dallas, TX 75235-0528
(214) 590-8807

Public Information Office
Harris County Juvenile Probation Department
3540 West Dallas
Houston, TX 77019
(713) 521-4122

Writers In The Schools
1515 Branard
Houston, TX 77006
(713) 523-3877

THERE ARE LOCAL ANTIVIOLENCE PROJECTS AROUND THE COUNTRY. IN YOUR HOMETOWN, THEY MAY BE SPONSORED BY THE BOYS AND GIRLS CLUBS OF AMERICA, THE YMCA, THE YWCA, A RAPE CRISIS CENTER, A COMMUNITY HOTLINE, A VICTIM SUPPORT GROUP, A YOUTH CENTER, OR A RELIGIOUS ORGANIZATION.

IF YOU WANT TO CONNECT WITH SUCH A GROUP, YOU WILL HAVE TO DO SOME RESEARCH. START BY LOOKING IN YOUR TELEPHONE DIRECTORY IN BOTH THE WHITE AND YELLOW PAGES UNDER THE NAME OF ONE OR MORE OF THESE GROUPS.

BOOKS

Here are two lists of books that are popular among incarcerated teenagers. The first was compiled by librarian Diana Tixier Herald, of Grand Junction, Colorado, who regularly visits a coed juvenile correctional facility. She writes about this experience in *School Library Journal*, May 1995.

The second was compiled by institutional librarian Stephan Likosky, Office of Special Services, New York, New York, who visits several facilities, including Rikers Island, through which twenty-five thousand juvenile offenders pass each year.

Carlson, Lori M., ed. *Cool Salsa: Bilingual Poems on Growing Up Latino in the United States.* New York: Holt, Rinehart, 1994.

Grant, Cynthia D. *Shadow Man.* New York: Atheneum, 1992.

Janeczko, Paul B. *Stardust 'Otel.* New York: Orchard Books, 1993.

McCall, Nathan. *Makes Me Wanna Holler.* New York: Random House, 1994.

Obstfeld, Raymond. *The Joker and the Thief.* New York: Delacorte Press, 1993.

Philbrick, Rodman. *Freak the Mighty.* Blue Sky Press/ Scholastic, 1993.

Shetterly, Will. *Nevernever.* San Diego: Harcourt, Brace, 1993.

Taylor, J. Clark. *The House that Crack Built.* San Francisco: Chronicle Books, 1992.

Augenbraum, Harold, and Ilan Stavans, eds. *Growing Up Latino.* Boston: Houghton Mifflin, 1993.

Brown, Claude. *Manchild in the Promised Land.* New York: Signet Books, 1965.

Childress, Alice. *A Hero Ain't Nothing but a Sandwich.* New York: Avon Books, 1982.

Goines, Donald. *Black Gangster.* Los Angeles: Holloway House, 1977.

———. *Black Girl Lost.* Los Angeles: Holloway House, 1973.

———. *Death List.* Los Angeles: Holloway House, 1974.

———. *Never Die Alone.* Los Angeles: Holloway House, 1974.

Gugliotta, Guy. *Kings of Cocaine.* New York: Simon and Schuster, 1989.

Malcolm X with Alex Haley. *The Autobiography of Malcolm X.* New York: Grove Press, 1965.

Movsesian, Ara John. *Pearls of Love: How to Write Love Letters and Love Poems.* Fresno, CA: Electric Press, 1983.

CONFUSING WORDS

HERE IS A LIST OF WORDS THAT ARE WELL KNOWN TO TEENAGERS INVOLVED IN THE JUVENILE JUSTICE SYSTEM BUT MAY BE CONFUSING TO THEIR PEERS OUTSIDE. THE DEFINITIONS WERE PROVIDED BY ASHLEY, AGE SIXTEEN, WHO IS CURRENTLY INCARCERATED IN A CLOSED-CUSTODY FACILITY.

closed custody: Being in closed custody means that you are locked in and don't have the freedom to make choices for yourself—such as when to come and go, when to eat, sleep, take a shower, do chores, etc. Life is structured for you by other people.

community service: Community service is often a sentence given as a way for you to "pay your dues" to society for what you have done. It is often called *restitution*. You may have to clean up an area in your city, for example. You will be doing something that gives back to the community in a positive way to make up for the negative things you have done.

corrections (juvenile): This is often referred to as simply *the system*. It includes the training schools, detentions, camp programs, shelter homes, parole and probation officers, and transition programs.

detention: Also known as *juvenile detention hall, juvenile detention center,* etc. Detention is like a time-out from society—a time and place to get juveniles to slow down and take a look at your behaviors. Detention is also a temporary holding place while awaiting sentencing for any crime you may have committed. It is a locked facility, which means many of your freedoms are lost due to your behaviors that got you into detention.

locked down: This can be a form of isolation, such as being locked down in your room. Being locked down is often a form of discipline within a training school or detention center. A juvenile is locked down until he or she can behave in an appropriate manner.

lockup: To be locked up means that you are in a facility where you don't have your rights or freedom any longer. It is not your choice to stay or go. Often the consequence of a crime is to be locked up in a training school or detention.

nark: Also known as a *mark, snitch, tattletale, rat, buster,* or *sidebuster.* It is defined as a person who tells on other people to get yourself out of trouble or to make yourself look good—known as earning "brownie points."

parole: A person is let out on parole after you have been in a locked facility for a long amount of time. Every parole agreement is different according to the specific needs of the person on parole. Violation of a parole agreement, which may result in the person on parole having to be put back into the locked facility, is called a parole revocation.

probation: Probation is often an alternative to being locked up in detention. It is looked at as a first step in punishment. Freedom is limited. Oftentimes juveniles are put on house arrest as a part of your probation. This means you may have to wear a bracelet that alerts police when you leave your house or you may have to call in at scheduled times throughout the day.

training school: A training school is the juvenile equivalent of adult prison, but that's not to say that you get the same treatment as adults. A training school involves learning new skills to deal with life effectively in society where you have messed up before. The doors are locked. When you leave, you are on parole.

DIRECT CONTACT

IF YOU HAVE ANY QUESTIONS OR COMMENTS, OR IF YOU FEEL LIKE SHARING LIFE EXPERIENCES ON THE ISSUE OF JUVENILE CRIME AND VIOLENCE, PLEASE CONTACT US:

Janet Bode/Stan Mack
c/o Delacorte Press
1540 Broadway
New York, New York 10036
E-mail: janbode@aol.com
stamack@aol.com

THANKS

The creation of this book took us on a long journey. We would like to thank our families and friends for help along the way: the Bodes, Barbara and Carolyn; the Macks, Pearl, Kenny, and Peter; and Linda Broessel, Kay Franey, Jane Goldberg, Harriet and Ted Gottfried, Ernie Lutze, Frieda Lutze, Carole Mayedo, Rosemarie and Marvin Mazor, Betty Medsger, Judy Pollock, Howie Rosen, Michael Sexton, and Deborah Udin.

The poetry found in the "Inside" section was written by youths incarcerated at the Juvenile Detention Center, the Burnett-Bayland Home, and Harris County Youth Village, institutions run by the Harris County Juvenile Probation Department, Houston, Texas. The teenagers' talents were developed with the encouragement of the faculty of Writers In The

Schools, Randall Watson, project coordinator. We thank them for their participation.

We also thank the staffs and youth offenders at the other facilities represented in these pages. Although they request anonymity, we want them to know we deeply appreciate their assistance. Without their efforts, and in the individual teenagers' cases the willingness to open their lives, this book would not exist.

The following people invited us into their homes, schools, libraries, and offices. They offered advice and counsel and often arranged for us to speak to students. They too contributed to making this book a memorable adventure. Without their involvement, the "Outside" section would have been incomplete. Thanks go to Agnes Beck, young-adult librarian, Andrew Heiskell Library for the Blind and Physically Handicapped, New York, New York; Gail Berendzen, president, Women of Washington, Washington, D.C.; Jan Christenson, media specialist, Park West High School, New York, New York; James E. Cook, young-adult specialist, Dayton and Montgomery County Public Library, Dayton, Ohio; Barbara Diment, media specialist, Missouri Association of School Librarians, Kansas City, Missouri; Susan Farber, young-adult/reference librarian, Chappaqua Public Library, Chappaqua, New York; Marilee Fogelsong, coordinator, young-adult services, and Mary Jane Tacchi, assistant coordinator,

New York Public Library, New York, New York; Julie Geis-Edsall, coeditor, *Inside Looking Out: Writings from the Heart of MonDay,* MonDay Community Correctional Institution, Dayton, Ohio; Harriet Gribben, humanities teacher, Coalition School for Social Change, New York, New York; Jane Hanson, English teacher, Metropolitan Learning Center, Portland, Oregon; Sharon Heinz, media specialist, Ruskin High School, Kansas City, Missouri; Marvin Hoffman, literature teacher, Jones High School, Houston, Texas; Jane Jury, media specialist, Elkton High School, Elkton, Maryland; Arlene Pearlman, coordinator, Bergen County Teen Arts Festival, Hackensack, New Jersey; Glenda Phipps, former teacher, The Osborne Association, Bronx, New York; the Honorable John Racanelli, Judicial Arbitration and Mediation Services, Inc., San Francisco, California; Joe Reid, assistant principal, Dilys Lande and Sharon Sorrels, media specialists, and Judith Shipley, language arts teacher, Benjamin Banneker High School, Washington, D.C.; Shayna Schneider, president, Mentors, Inc., Washington, D.C.; Patricia Shea-Bischoff, conference coordinator, New York State Reading Association, Albany, New York; Ann Sparanese, head, adult and young-adult services, Englewood Public Library, Englewood, New Jersey; Eugenie Stahl and Linda Kiperman, Queens Literacy Project, Board of Education, Brooklyn, New York; Glenda Swaffar, media specialist, Hickman Mill High School, Kansas City,

Missouri; Arlene Weber Morales, media specialist, Marine Park School, IS 278, Brooklyn, New York; and Susan Wilson and Donna Harley, media specialists, Elmont Memorial High School, Elmont, New York.

And, finally, a special thank-you to Kelly Boundy and our support system at BDD—Delacorte Press, especially Beverly Horowitz, Kathy Squires, and Judith Haut.

JANET BODE writes hard-hitting nonfiction for and about teenagers. Through group discussions and one-on-one interviews, she uncovers the personal stories behind today's headlines and then reports them—along with survival strategies—to her readers. Several of her books, including *Heartbreak and Roses: Real Life Stories of Troubled Love, The Voices of Rape: Healing the Hurt, New Kids on the Block: Oral Histories of Immigrant Teens,* and *Beating the Odds: Stories of Unexpected Achievers,* have been selected as ALA Best Books for Young Adults. Her book *Different Worlds: Interracial and Cross-Cultural Dating* was made into a CBS-TV *Schoolbreak Special. Hard Time* is her twelfth young-adult book.

STAN MACK is a reporter-cartoonist and creator of the weekly comics *Real Life Funnies* and *Out-Takes.* Besides working with Janet Bode, he is the author of *Stan Mack's Real Life American Revolution* and a popular picture book, *Ten Bears in My Bed.* He is at work on other graphic history books for adults and teens.